Genetic Jihad

James R. Campbell

Writers Club Press
San Jose New York Lincoln Shanghai

Genetic Jihad

Published by Writers Club Press
an imprint of iUniverse.com, Inc.

For information address:
iUniverse.com, Inc.
620 North 48th Street
Suite 201
Lincoln, NE 68504-3467
www.iuniverse.com

ISBN: 0-595-09817-7

Printed in the United States of America

Chapter 1

Teddy Medway couldn't believe his luck. This was a unique piece of medical history. The long months of examining, translating and interpreting the old German medical records had revealed many examples of incredible and bizarre human experimentation. Medical historians like he had known for decades that Nazi scientists, working with prisoners in concentration camps, had used people like laboratory animals. However records of this work had been sealed since the War, unavailable for examination. Many people violently opposed what they considered publicity for the accomplishments of these murderous, amoral Nazi researchers. Others, though condemning the actions and spirit of the scientists involved, still wanted to examine the findings critically and objectively. Could anything be learned from this travesty that could benefit mankind?

Medway's Doctor of Philosophy degree from Oxford depended on an analysis of these records. His father, Nelson Medway, Deputy Minister of Education for Medicine, had used all his political clout in London and called in all his diplomatic cards in Germany to get permission for his son to go through the National Archives and study the documents. After two years of legal and political wrangling Medway has succeeded, and Teddy was spending sixteen hours a day going through volumes of handwritten patient records and laboratory notebooks.

As his thesis was a study of the moral and social implications of human experimentation, he had tried to put aside the experiments themselves and develop a picture of the men and women who had done the work. However one particular set of experiments performed at Dachau in

1941-42 had drawn him deep into the experimental details. Nazi doctors there had conducted treatment trials in which prisoners were first infected with a strain of bacteria that was known to cause mild illness, then treated with various experimental drugs. An unexpected complication of these experiments was that many of the Jewish prisoners infected with the bacteria suffered serious illness. Some even failed completely to respond to therapy, became paralyzed and died of respiratory failure. However, other non-Jewish prisoners of war suffered only mild illness and recovered completely, even without drugs. So it suggested to Medway that a genetic component might have been involved. He also knew from his Microbiology courses that the bacteria used in the experiments produced a mild toxin that affected the enzyme acetylcholinesterase. This enzyme is essential in nervous transmission because it releases the neurotransmitter acetylcholine, or ACH, from its receptor on nerve cells after a nervous impulse has passed, to prevent the continuous transmission of nervous signals. If ACH remains bound to its receptor, nervous transmission continues without interruption, leading to sustained muscular contraction, paralysis and death. Although the Nazi scientists did not understand the results at the time, it appeared quite clear to Medway that at least a subset of ethnic Jews must possess an altered ACH esterase that was exquisitely sensitive to the action of the bacterial toxin.

The more Medway studied the experiments the more he found himself struggling with the same debate that had nearly prevented his examining the records in the first place. The experiments appeared to reveal an example of genetic hypersensitivity to a toxin with anti-cholinesterase activity, and perhaps to anticholinesterase compounds in general. This could have significant impact on medicine, particularly in the area of anesthesiology and in neurological disorders. Despite the significance of these findings, he was repelled by the researchers' methods, by their total disregard for human life. More importantly, however, he somehow felt he had stumbled upon information he just should not know—that no one should know.

Now half a century after the original experiments were completed, Medway was experiencing them, and he felt an indescribable foreboding. There was danger here, so real he found himself looking over his shoulder in the solitude of the locked research room. As the classic German script grudgingly shared its secrets with him, he envisioned the laboratories, heard the screams and saw the shroud-covered results of "failed" experiments being wheeled out on carts for disposal.

One evening at MacReady's, a local hangout for Oxford students, he discussed his problem with a fellow graduate student, Nayah Salim. Nayah had come to London four years ago with her father, a Lebanese diplomat, and she was already nearing completion of her doctoral degree in Microbiology. A very private person, Nayah had developed no close friendships at Oxford, but she listened intently as Teddy confided in her. Her obsessive commitment to her work, along with a series of brilliant discoveries in genetic engineering of microorganisms, had earned her the nickname of "Nobel Nayah," a title she shrugged off with a Mona Lisa smile. She was intensely interested in the experimental findings Medway described, but less so in his moral dilemma. When he concluded that he simply could not continue and that he must destroy the data he had accumulated, Nayah exploded.

"Destroy the data? You cannot! This is historic. Think what this can mean if we work on this together!"

Teddy was more than surprised at the intensity of her response. He had never seen Nayah so agitated. As he tried to explain why he felt the data must never be made public, he watched her frustration turn to anger. Looking in her dark eyes he saw something ominous and frightening.

"You idiot," she hissed venomously, "you little idiot."

She was only one person speaking, but her voice appeared to Medway to be ten thousand. Heads were beginning to turn at nearby tables, and Teddy quickly shoved his notes into his briefcase, excusing himself.

"I have to go back to the library and think, Nayah," he said. "I'll talk to you later."

Later that evening, still struggling with the decision to release his findings or not, Teddy walked slowly down the narrow cobblestone path behind the library. As he passed one of the gnarled oak trees that lined the path he was startled to see Nayah step out in front of him.

"Nayah," he said, "what are..."

He only noticed a glint of metal in her hand before a sharp noise and a blinding white light in his brain ended the conversation. Recovering Medway's briefcase full of data, the microbiologist disappeared silently into the night.

By the next morning, Nayah was on a Lebanese Air flight out of Heathrow, heading for Beirut. The airsickness was worse than ever, as her body struggled with yet another infection. Since being diagnosed with AIDS two years before, she had redoubled her efforts to learn everything she could about molecular biology. Her friends and family told her she was crazy for continuing to work in microbiology, with her immune system so weakened. To her it was an obsession, but it was not madness. Four years earlier, while vacationing in the United States with her father in St. Louis, she had been seriously injured in an automobile accident. Rushed to the nearest hospital, Washington Jewish Hospital of St. Louis, she had received nearly five units of whole blood during surgery. Unknown to her or the hospital staff, the blood was tainted with the deadly human immunodeficiency virus and now, four years later, she was dying of AIDS. She was a zombie, the living dead, and the Jewish doctors had killed her.

Revenge had seduced her slowly. She resisted it at first, it was irrational, but it persisted. There was no answer to "Why?" There was no one to blame but "them." Bitter that her own death was inevitable and beyond her control, Nayah had mastered the skills to create "designer-death" for others, and now she had her target. Her body functioned, but her soul was dead, and in death she had become liberated. She felt allegiance to no one–not family, not friends, not country. Like a precisely engineered machine, she worked towards a precise goal, to kill her killers.

Chapter 2

The hills were just appearing against the eastern sky as Laini shouldered the two large water buckets and started down the rocky path to the spring. An American citizen with a business degree from Cornell, she smiled as she reflected on her situation. Her family in New York had urged her not to go to Israel at this time, citing the potential negative effects on her career and the danger from Moslem terrorists. Laini had always been a rebel, and a two-year hiatus at Tafiz Kibbutz would give her time to reexamine some basic values in her life. She would never see another dawn.

Ahmad Nabul was already back among the olive and acacia trees of Jordan, far from the Israeli-patrolled buffer zone, by the time dawn spread over the West Bank. Though well out of danger he ran hard, his heart pounding. His mission had been a success. Perfectly planned and executed, his lone foray into enemy territory in the middle of the night had accomplished its goal without detection. The only Israeli patrol he encountered, five young soldiers smoking cigarettes and making enough noise to be heard half a kilometer away, had passed by his crouched form a scant three meters away.

"Dogs!" he thought. "Soon the only noise they will be making is a death rattle."

Laini was glad to set the buckets down. Her daily jogs through Central Park had obviously not conditioned her for 500-yard uphill hikes, carrying fifty pounds of water. Keeping the camp cistern full was her job though, and the spring was the only source of water for the sixty residents in the settlement. She laughed with the other women as she topped off the water in the cement cistern. Although they understood her, the Israelis were openly amused by her American accent. *I'll bet they think all Americans are from the Bronx,* she thought, as she poured the remaining water from the bucket into her mouth. It was cool and good, and she carelessly spilled some down her neck, soaking the Big Red logo on her T-shirt.

Back at the base camp, Nabul celebrated with the others. Soon the Zionists would know the true power of Jihad. Soon the whole world would know. For now however he was an instrument, a small but critical component in a grand, holy plan. Nabul was a fanatic but he was also a professional, and he did not like not knowing more about the weapon he had employed. He liked even less the rumors he had heard that the "poison" had been manufactured by the Russians.

The entire operation had been held under such secrecy that Nabul had not been informed of the actual date or target of the strike until the day before. A few days earlier however, an incredible rumor had somehow leaked out among the Shiite fighters that Russian scientists had developed for the Hezbollah some sort of new poison that killed only Jews. So it was a true honor that he and his small group had been entrusted with the first field deployment of this weapon. Nabul had prayed fervishly that night, willingly committing his life to the success of the mission. So, laughing and feasting with the others, he relished the almost unexpected result that he had returned alive.

At Tafiz, Emunah Moyen was the first. Returning from midnight security rounds, her son-in-law had found the old woman on the floor beside her bed, gasping for breath.

"Ana come quickly," he shouted, "your mother is ill!" Daniel silently cursed himself for agreeing to let Emunah move in with them at the

Kibbutz. Until the birth of their daughter he had held firm against the idea, but when little Abi arrived Emunah had redoubled her efforts.

"I want to be with my granddaughter before I die," she had pleaded.

"Well, she is getting her wish," he thought grimly.

The old ham radio in the parlor worked passably, but Daniel knew it would be pointless to call for help. The nearest medical facility was the small clinic at Hebruk, two hours away over a dangerous, ill-maintained dirt road. The authorities would not risk sending their only doctor out at night for an old woman who would be dead from a heart attack before he arrived. Daniel laid Emunah gently in her bed and knelt with Ana to pray for her mother. It was almost dawn when Ana rose unsteadily to her feet.

"I must go outside," she said.

"Do you want me to go with you?" he asked.

"No, I'll be alright. I just need some air."

Sitting against the bedroom wall, Daniel dozed for nearly an hour, when a scream shocked him awake. Groggily rushing out the door, he stumbled over his wife's body. The scream came again, from a house three doors away. Daniel tried to stand, but he was disoriented and fell drunkenly to his knees. He could hardly breathe.

"What is happening?" he croaked, as the morning sky went dark.

The driver of the patrol jeep cursed and hit the brake as he swerved to miss the body lying in the road. The jeep skidded wildly in the gravel, hung for an instant on two wheels and landed heavily on its right side. Dazed, the three soldiers extricated themselves from their vehicle.

"Anybody hurt?" called Sergeant Renna. The Sergeant, a veteran of five years service in the occupied territories, moved quickly to the body in the road.

"Dead." he stated flatly. It was certainly not the first time he had seen a dead person. "Hey, wait a minute," he said. "I know this kid. This is Jonah Siemen's son, from Tafiz."

"There's his bike," shouted Private Daken, pointing at the small Husquvarna on its side in the dirt. "He must have crashed last night some time."

Examining the young form, Sergeant Renna noticed something peculiar. Other than a few minor scratches there was no hint of trauma or any serious injury. His eyes quickly scanned the nearby hills, searching for danger he felt but could not define. "Let's get the jeep back up," directed Renna, "and put the body in the back. Daken, radio Command and tell them we are going to Tafiz."

As they rounded the last curve into the settlement the Sergeant barked, "Hold it!" Automatically flipping the safety off his Uzi, Renna quickly scanned the village. It was ten in the morning and no one was in view. "Daken, check out that group of houses on the left," he whispered. "I'll move down by the meeting house. Yoel, you cover us from this position. Keep your eyes and ears open."

Private Yeol Weiss, a city boy from Tel-Aviv, nervously gripped the 50-caliber as he watched the two khaki-clad figures disappear behind the nearest structures.

"Sergeant," came Private Daken's excited voice, "I have found that American girl. I think she's...dead."

"Dammit," the Sergeant cursed to himself as he heard Daken's cry. "Why doesn't he just tell the world we are here."

In less than half an hour Sergeant Renna had confirmed what he had tried to deny from the moment he entered Tafiz, in fact from the moment his patrol had found the young boy out on the road. The residents of the Kibbutz had been massacred. The only survivor Renna found was one-month old Abi Mizrahi. Cradled in the soldier's strong arms, the infant cried piteously as she hungrily probed his chest for the warm breast that would never be found. Gripping the radio transmitter with his free hand, Renna slowly and deliberately called in a terse report. "Command, this is Unit Six. Red Rocket. I repeat, Red Rocket."

In five years with the border security detachment he had never had occasion to use the Red Rocket code, and with good reason. A Red Rocket message cut through all protocol, all bureaucratic hurdles, and was relayed directly to the Office of the Minister of Defense. Renna did not hesitate in his decision because he correctly sensed that what he and his men had found at Tafiz was something far greater than a military matter.

Defense Minister Shoram was concluding a briefing with his military Chiefs of Staff when his aide, apologizing for the interruption, delivered the Red Rocket. The DM impatiently opened the sealed message, noted the code word and dismissed the aide. "Ask General Morah to meet me in my office immediately. Gentlemen, thank you for the briefing. That will be all."

The senior officers came to attention as Shoram rose and turned toward the door connecting the conference room with his office. Their exchanged glances betrayed puzzlement over a message that required the immediate attention of the DM and the Chief of Intelligence, yet was apparently not for their eyes.

Barely three minutes later, General Benjamin Morah knocked on the Defense Minister's door.

"Come in Ben, have a seat," said the DM. "What do you make of this?" he asked, as he handed the message to the General. The CI scrutinized the message for a few seconds before his eyes raised to lock on Shoram's.

"What evidence is there that this was a CBW attack?"

"Nothing hard yet," answered Shoram, "except that there are sixty men, women and children dead without a scratch, in one of our border settlements."

"The Emergency Reaction Team…" started Morah.

"Already alerted," interrupted the DM. "Should be on their way in minutes. Ben, I'd like you to meet the specialists from Lab Five out at Tafiz and assess the situation personally."

"Yes, Sir," replied Morah. "Do I have permission to take our new sensors to the scene?"

The Defense Minister hesitated. "Yes, go ahead. This is what we developed those systems for." It was a Top Secret capability that was essential for Israel's defense, but one which the Minister had hoped would never be needed. He almost feared the answer they could give. Lab Five, the "Black Lab," whose existence was known to fewer than twenty people outside of the laboratory, was where Israel's program in Chemical and Biological Warfare Defense was carried out. "I want a preliminary report on my desk by 1800, and Ben," the DM paused, "be careful. We don't know what were getting into here."

Major Mordechai Samuels was going over the latest scenario for a hypothetical CBW attack on Israel his staff had prepared for his review when the FLASH message came in on his personal secure teletype. It took him a few seconds to realize that this was not just another drill. Stabbing an intercom button, he ordered, "David, I want to see you immediately." Young for a major at thirty-one, Samuel's doctoral degree from the Weizmann Institute with dual concentrations in Biochemistry and Molecular Genetics had allowed him to start his compulsory military service in the rank of Captain. He was assigned to the research and development component of the Army's Extraordinary Defensive Measures Unit. The work in the EDM group fascinated him, where fourteen-hour workdays soon became routine. Samuel's publications list already surpassed that of most senior university professors but the classification level of his work kept virtually all of his reports out of the public domain. Now, four years later, he held the rank of Major and the position of head of Israel's Emergency Reaction Team. The ERT consisted of military scientists and engineers whose job was to form the first defensive response to a CBW attack on Israel. On more than one occasion, proposed cuts in defense spending had threatened the entire program. Major Samuels had little tolerance for the bureaucrats who proposed the cuts and who simply did not accept the possibility of a CBW attack on their country. Ever since the age of eighteen, when a car bomb in front of his parents' store in downtown Haifa had orphaned him and his sister, Samuels knew that anything was possible.

"Yes, Sir?" asked Captain Steinberg as he stepped into the office.

"Come in, David, and close the door," said Samuels. "We have a Charlie Bravo Two at Tafiz, a new settlement about twenty kilometers from Hebruk."

Steinberg's eyes widened for an instant then recovered, as he absorbed the information. This was not a drill. "Charlie Bravo Two" was the code for an unconfirmed but strongly suspected CBW attack. His Commander would never joke on this subject. "Right. The Team will be on the chopper in five minutes."

Chapter 3

"Zack, the telephone's for you. It's General Carter's office," Sally Rawlins called from the cabin porch.

"Shit," he muttered, setting his fishing gear down on the dock as he turned back up the path, away from the lake. Colonel Zachary Rawlins, whose second home was the Pentagon, served as a senior consultant in the Department of Defense Biotechnology Assessment Program, and he and his wife were just beginning the first of fourteen days of well deserved vacation away from the pulse of the nation. Now, what was unquestionably to have been the finest bass fishing day in the history of Green Lake, deep in the Vermont mountains, was about to self-destruct. Zack was angry at himself, for naively assuming that the emergency telephone number he had dutifully recorded on his leave papers would never be used.

"Thanks!" he snapped inappropriately at his wife, grabbing the receiver. Taking a deep breath, and exhaling slowly, he said in his most professional voice, "Yes, Sir, General, this is Colonel Rawlins. What can I do for you, Sir?"

"Aw, cut the 'Sir' crap, Zack. This is Monty," came the amused reply.

"Monty! What the hell? This better be important. I've got a world record bass just waiting..."

"Hold it, Zack, hold it," said the General's aide. "Carter told me to call you. He thinks the Israelis had a little problem a few days ago and he wants you back in D.C. right away."

"A few days ago? Thinks? That's some intelligence report, pal," growled Rawlins.

"You know I can't give you any details over the phone," said Lieutenant Colonel Rodriguez, "but this one's hot and you better get back here ASAP."

Replacing the receiver, Rawlins turned toward his wife.

"Well, it's been fun," sighed Sally Rawlins, as she read the message in his eyes. Twenty years experience as an Army wife had honed her intuition to where she just...knew.

Zack's guts tightened and his face flushed as his wife turned and walked quietly into the bedroom, closing the door behind her. He wanted to grab her arm, to stop her and tell her how important she was to him, but he couldn't. The fact was this mission was more important to him than his wife, and they both knew it. At that moment, he couldn't even tell her he loved her, because it would only sound cheap and insincere.

Inside the bedroom, Sally dug through the jumble of cosmetics in the bottom of her makeup box to find the two bottles of Prozac and Valium. She shook three of each into her trembling palm and, with a furtive look back toward the door, popped the pills into her mouth. A sympathetic family practitioner in Arlington kept Sally fortified with a regular supply of the drugs to combat her depression and relieve her stress, and Zack knew nothing of it. She could no longer tell if the pills were widening the gap between her and her husband, or if the distance between them was causing her to depend on the pills. She only knew that for a few hours, things would be a little better.

Defense Minister Shoram's sphincters tightened as he clenched General Morah's situation report. The clipped, military style of the message made the contents all the more chilling. Area secured. Sixty casualties. One survivor—female, one month old. Perimeter control established to restrict entrance/egress. Biocontainment level P4 implemented to protect personnel and contain bodies and samples. Lab Five helo transferring bodies to secure examination area at Meda Air Force Base. Sergeant Renna team and surviving resident evacuated to hospital isolation room at same. Lab Five sensors detect no, repeat no, BW agents at scene. Environmental samples negative for CW agents. Analysis: Offensive CBW attack, 60 casualties; attackers unknown; agent(s) employed unknown; Lab Five following up with further detailed analysis at home base.

"No microbial agent? No evidence of a toxin? Nothing?" demanded the Defense Minister.

"No, Sir," replied Major Samuels. His team at Lab Five had just completed two days of round-the-clock testing of the samples from Tafiz. "Even the ADP was negative."

"ADP?" asked Shomar. He had heard the term but didn't fully understand the technology.

"The ADP—Amplified DNA Probe—is the most sensitive diagnostic assay Lab Five has developed," explained Samuels. "In fact, it's the most sensitive bioassay in existence. A few years ago an American group discovered an extremely efficient DNA synthesizing enzyme called a polymerase. We used this enzyme to develop a method for amplifying DNA, the unique informational molecules of any living organism, a billion fold in under three hours. That kind of amplification of the target gives us the sensitivity to detect the presence of a single pathogen in a sample. So far though, no luck. We're still running down a few CW possibilities and I'll report back the moment we have the results."

The mood in Lab Five was somber. This was their mission, their only mission—to rapidly detect CBW agents and advise the DM on countermeasures—and they had no answers.

"Anything?" asked Major Samuels hopefully, after returning from the DM's office.

"Not yet," replied Steinberg. "We used the ADP on our complete panel of BW agents. We've checked blood samples, soil samples, water samples. I've used up over a year's supply of my test reagents already."

"You found nothing at all in the water supply?" asked the Major.

"Nothing other than the usual crud. You know, some *Pseudomonas*, a lot of *E. coli*," answered Steinberg.

A high coliform count...thought the Major. Coliform bacteria, including *Escherichia coli*, in a water sample indicated fecal contamination of the water supply. These bacteria were normal inhabitants of the human and animal gut, and virtually everywhere in the environment, but were rarely associated with severe disease. *However*...

"I know what you're thinking, Major," said Steinberg. "Engineered bacteria. We checked that, too. Negative for foreign tox genes." The normally innocuous *E. coli* was the laboratory darling of genetic engineers, who in the last decade had spliced into it literally hundreds of genes from different organisms, enabling the bacteria to manufacture and release an equally broad array of foreign proteins. So it would have been a relatively simple matter to "weaponize" *E. coli* by engineering into it a gene that encoded a lethal toxin.

"You read my mind better than my wife," observed Samuels with thinly disguised irritation. Captain Steinberg was a world-class molecular biologist, and the EDM group was very fortunate to have him, but it chafed Samuels to realize that the Captain thought of him as the "Old Man," who needed to have things spelled out.

"Probably some donkey just crapped in the spring," quipped Steinberg. "On the other hand," his face turning grim, "donkey turds don't kill."

"I'm afraid you're right," agreed Samuels. He considered the Captain's tendency toward vulgarity rather unbecoming of an officer but he had to admit, the man knew how to make a point. "Get the *E. coli* isolate on the Multiplex. I want a complete sequence of that bug's chromosome."

Steinberg didn't even flinch. Ever since Lab Five got their Multispectral Multiplex DNA Sequencer, "the Multiplex," operational a year ago, DNA analysis had become almost a trivial exercise. The Multiplex included sophisticated robotics, which virtually eliminated human error, and a new integrated circuit chip, the Femtosecond Signal Processor. The FSP was a "smart" chip that could be programmed to look for similarities and patterns in DNA sequence data, thus eliminating the need to identify each individual "base," or subunit, in the DNA. This was a major technological breakthrough, and projects that just two years ago would have taken ten man-years were now reduced to merely several day's work. With a Multiplex, DNA analysis could be accomplished almost as routinely as a simple blood-glucose or liver function test.

The equipment represented hardware that was on the Controlled Technology List of the United States, but Israel had managed to obtain it as part of a new CBW defense pact between the two countries. Apart from these two countries, only Britain and Japan were approved for Multiplex technology. The biotech watchdogs in the U.S. Congress had enacted legislation that made it virtually impossible for nations that sponsored terrorism, and non-U.S. allies in general, to obtain this equipment. The information such technology could provide opened the door for major advances in human health care, but it also held the potential for great harm.

Zack pulled into the driveway of his home in Alexandria, Virginia, at ten o'clock that night, after driving straight through from Vermont. While Sally began extracting the jumble of clothes and camping equipment that had been hurriedly tossed in the back of their Volvo stationwagon, Zack sprinted into the house to call General Carter. He was a little disappointed, though not particularly surprised, to hear the gruff voice after a single ring of the phone.

"Carter."

"Yes, Sir, General. Colonel Rawlins. I'm just dropping Sally off at home and I'll be right over."

Ten minutes later Rawlins pulled into the Pentagon's underground parking lot, taking one of the ten spaces marked "Flag/General Officers Only" near the main entrance.

"Why not?" he thought. "Fat chance of ten Flags coming in this late. Besides, Carter will cover for me."

Inside, the Marine guard eyed him suspiciously, and carefully scrutinized his I.D. card. It suddenly dawned on Rawlins that he probably looked more like a homeless street person than a U.S. Army Colonel. He hadn't shaved, or even removed his fishing hat. The stone-faced young Corporal was not a bit impressed by the hat's collection of lures and flies, despite the fact that each item was a miniature medal testifying to some memorable piscatorial exploit. The Marine would undoubtedly have been more impressed with the nine rows of ribbons that Rawlins normally wore on his chest when entering the Pentagon under other circumstances.

The negative G's in the express elevator told him he had arrived at the fifth floor. Hurrying down the corridor, Rawlins came to the imposing mahogany door labeled "Deputy Chief of Intelligence," where he paused momentarily to equilibrate. He straightened the collar of his Pendelton and picked some lint off the front, as if it would make a difference, before knocking twice on the door.

The door responded with a dull buzz, as the electronic lock disengaged. Rawlins shoved the heavy door open and stepped into the plush office, where General Carter sat reclining in his desk chair behind the usual cloud of cigar smoke.

"Sit down, Zack," ordered the General.

Zack did as he was told then watched, bemused, as a thick smoke screen was laid down between them. He often wondered if the cigar were a tactic the DCI had developed in his political dealings or whether he simply had a passion for good Havanas. Waiting respectfully for the General to speak, Zack wondered to himself if Castro ever planted "bugs" in boxes of expensive Cuban cigars for export.

"The Israelis got hit with a CBW attack last Thursday, and have asked for our help," stated Carter. "I want you to go over there and find out who is responsible and why Lab Five can't I.D. the agent. Minister Shoram and his cabinet are real pissed and if they don't get some answers soon, the hawks in their defense ministry may convince him to nuke half the Middle East." General Carter certainly had a way of communicating the urgency of a situation.

"I'll call the Duty Officer to get a flight..." started Rawlins.

"Don't bother," interrupted Carter. "You're on United 106 out of Dulles at 0730. Go get some sleep. A car will be by at 0530, and I'm afraid you can't tell Sally anything."

"Yes, Sir," replied Rawlins, rising to leave. "I'll call you from Tel Aviv."

"Humph," acknowledged the DCI, his attention already shifting back to his message traffic. "Oh, and Zack," he added without looking up, "nice hat."

As Zack stepped out of the office his stomach tightened. His sister Elizabeth, and her four-year-old daughter Sarah had planned on going to Israel for a vacation. If he recalled correctly, they were leaving their home in California for Tel Aviv today or tomorrow. Feeling suddenly helpless, his mind raced. How could he contact Elizabeth? Had they already left? Sarah's beautiful little face, with her big brown eyes appeared as he envisioned the two of them walking into a BW attack in Tel Aviv. His anxious call to his sister's home in Los Angeles was greeted with a cheery recorded message. "She's gone," he whispered in frustration. How would he ever have time to track her down in Tel Aviv, while on his mission?

Chapter 4

"Welcome to Tel Aviv, Colonel Rawlins," smiled the young officer at the VIP customs counter. "I'm Lieutenant Berman. I have a car waiting outside. We are to meet Minister Shoram at his office in 45 minutes."

"My bags..." started Rawlins.

"Taken care of, Sir. Everything is taken care of."

One thing about the Israelis, they sure were efficient when they wanted to be. For a Palestinian student, Israeli airport customs could mean a two-hour process including a strip search, but for a U.S. Army Intelligence officer it was only a brief walk directly from the plane to a car.

"Lieutenant, my sister, Elizabeth Miller and four year old niece are vacationing in Tel Aviv. I believe they are staying at the Intercontinental Hotel. Could you please get her in contact with me?"

"Roger that, Sir."

It was mid-morning and traffic was light as they drove quickly to National Defense Headquarters. Approaching the main gate of the compound, Lieutenant Berman flashed a red-bordered I.D. card at the guard, who snapped a salute that Rawlins could hear with the windows up.

Minister Shoram's office was on the top floor of the new, ten-story Central Planning Facility. After passing three separate checkpoints, the two presented themselves at the desk of Mrs. Raebel. Arielle Raebel, the Minister's secretary, was the final and unquestionably the most daunting challenge any terrorist would ever face in attempting to attack the DM. Two hundred pounds if she were an ounce, Arielle had survived five Defense Ministers and looked ready for five more.

"Do you have an appointment?" she snapped.

Of course they had an appointment. No one saw the DM without an appointment. More precisely, no one saw the DM unless they were in *Arielle's* appointment book.

Humoring her, Berman answered, "Yes, Ma'am, 10:45 I believe." Feeling a little testy himself, the Lieutenant decided to bring the pleasantries to a close. "What a lovely dress you're wearing this morning, Mrs. Raebel." *Twentieth century rummage sale,* he thought. It produced the desired effect. To the Reubenesque Mrs. Raebel any compliment was a conspiratorial falsehood, and it was like squeezing lemon juice into a paper cut.

"Go in. The Minister is expecting you."

"Zack," called the DM, smiling broadly as he shoved his hand across the huge mahogany desk, "you're looking well."

"And you, Sir," replied Rawlins, "perhaps a little more gray hair around the temples?"

The three men laughed as the Minister, rubbing his hand over his nearly bald head, quipped, "At my age I'll take it any way I can get it. That will be all, Lieutenant. Thank you."

The Minister's smile disappeared as the aide closed the door behind him.

"I'm glad General Carter could send you, Zack. We have a big problem on the West Bank, in fact, two big problems. As you know, four days ago an entire settlement was wiped out, and Lab Five thinks it was BW."

"And the second problem?" asked Rawlins.

"We can't I.D. the agent. Major Samuels' gene jockeys have tried everything in their bag of tricks but so far, nothing. I'm trying to keep a lid on things here while the EDM group comes up with some answers, but Rorsha and his boys have already fixed bayonets."

Zev Rorsha, the powerful chairman of the Special Military Security Committee and a former Colonel in the Israeli Palmach forces, was a perpetual thorn in Shoram's side. Rorsha was feared by the liberals in the

Likud almost as much as he was feared by the terrorists he relentlessly and mercilessly stalked.

"Has anyone taken credit for the attack?" asked Rawlins.

"Of course," replied Shomar. "Half a dozen of the usual two-bit fringe groups...plus a new one calling themselves "Fath," or "Victory.""

"What do you know about this Fath group?" inquired Rawlins. He had heard that name before, somewhere.

"Precious little. They first surfaced six months ago in connection with a RPG attack on a bus outside of Nablus. Survivors reported the attackers just stood there laughing while the bus burned, roasting twelve people trapped inside. They have no base that we know of and their leadership is unknown. One thing we know for sure—they're deadly."

Fath, thought Rawlins. *Where did I...*His concentration was snapped by the intercom buzz.

"What is it?" growled Shomar at his secretary. The Minister had learned that the best defense against Mrs. Raebel's acid personality was a strong offense.

"Major Samuels to see you, Sir," came the curt reply.

"Send him in."

Moments later the door swung open and the head of the ERT hurried in.

"Good Morning, Minister Shoram. Colonel Rawlins, what a surprise! Good to see you, Sir."

"Mordechai. So they've got you beat this time, eh?" goaded Rawlins.

The pained reaction in Samuels' eyes betrayed frustration, and Rawlins immediately wished he could take back his words.

"Not beat, Sir," challenged the Major with controlled defiance, "just very busy. We do have some interesting findings, but I'm afraid we don't yet know quite what they mean. We found an unusually high concentration of *E. coli* at Tafiz—both in the spring and in the camp cistern. More importantly, perhaps, we isolated the same *E. coli* from every one of the victims we checked so far. We weren't particularly excited about that at first, *E. coli* being such an ubiquitous organism, but we ran the bug on the

Multiplex anyway. The first thing we found was that it was the K-12 strain of *E. coli.*"

"K-12," interrupted Rawlins, "that's the common laboratory strain of *E. coli* used in genetic engineering."

"Correct," replied Samuels. "We then programmed the Multiplex to look for and sequence the *E. coli* tox gene."

"But you already know K-12 has the *E. coli* tox gene," protested Rawlins, "and that it only produces a very mild toxin with slight anti-cholinesterase activity."

"Correct again, and the DNA sequence we found was 99% identical to the published sequence of the K-12 gene. However, we found three mutations in the DNA of the Tafiz isolate, which would result in three amino acid substitutions in the toxin product from these particular bacteria."

"And…?" asked Rawlins.

"And that's where we need help," sighed Samuels. "We need some high-powered molecular modeling to determine the structure of the mutated toxin, and predict what effects the changes might have on the function of the molecule."

"How about Dr. Dan Reynolds at Cal-Tech?" offered Rawlins. "He's done a lot of excellent work for the U.S. DOD in the past, and his modeling group is hooked up to their own Cray II. They've got more computational firepower than anybody I know. If you concur, Minister Shoram, I could take Major Samuels' DNA sequence back with me and ask Reynolds to work it up."

"I don't know, Zack," hesitated the DM. "We do need the data immediately, but we can't tell your Dr. Reynolds anything about why we really need this information, or why we need it so fast."

"You could just tell him we've got some patients who are not responding to treatment," suggested Samuels, "and you need to determine if the mutations in this isolate could be the reason."

Not responding to treatment, Rawlins noted dryly. *Corpses usually don't.*

After a moment's consideration, the DM nodded his head, "Do it."

"Right," said Samuels, "I'll ask Dov to make a disk copy tonight that you can take back tomorrow, Colonel." Dov Messer, Lab Five's newest employee, was their computer expert. His professional credentials were so strong that he had been offered six-figure salaries by private corporations around the world. So when he had turned those down to remain in Israel and apply for a position in defense research, Personnel Acquisitions had bent all the rules to hire him. The intensive background investigation of Dov Messer had come up clean, except that as a student at Haifa University, Dov had been a member of a student activist group supporting new settlements in the occupied territories. His proactive concern for the security of Israel got him arrested three times, while trying to block the eviction of Jewish settlers. As Dov's reputation in the field of computers grew, he re-directed his energies to protecting Israel by making its computerized defense systems invincible.

In his six months on board, as Assistant Director of Computer Operations, Messer had installed over a million dollars worth of hardware upgrades, networked all the military intelligence agencies into Lab Five and orchestrated the "retirement" of half a dozen "1990's-thinking" systems programmers and engineers. His microscopic supervision of every phase of computer operations irritated some of the employees, but no one could deny that things were far more efficient now than before his arrival. In deference to the Director, Messer had declined a spacious suite in the building's penthouse, in favor of a small office off the main machine room, where he could be found working late nearly every night.

"Thanks, Mordechai," said Rawlins.

"Yes, Major, good job," added the DM. "I'll let you know as soon as we get the modeling data. Keep me informed of any new developments. That will be all."

"Minister Shoram, may I see the file on Fath?" asked Rawlins as the door shut behind Samuels.

"Of course," said the DM, pulling a thin manila folder marked "Top Secret" out of his top desk drawer. Compared to the file cabinets full of data Israeli intelligence had on groups like Hezbollah and Islamic Jihad, the pitiful collection of reports and documents on Fath seemed almost useless. Leafing through the pages, it suddenly came to Rawlins.

Fath. Over a year ago, routine HUMINT, or Human Intelligence, gathered by British agents in the Middle East had turned up a new, radical political group by that name. As most such new groups had only a few members, who were often only disgruntled visionaries split off from some existing radical group, they were noted but largely ignored by the British Intelligence organization M-5. The Fath report had come across Rawlins' desk via the CIA, which shared HUMINT with M-5, because of the statement, "It is believed Fath agents are being sent to the U.S. or U.K. for advanced training in science, particularly in chemistry and biotechnology."

"Why advanced training?" he had puzzled. "You certainly don't need a Ph.D. in Chemistry to stick a detonator into some Plastique, and why Biotechnology? Biological weapons?" The thought was chilling, and it also angered him. The U.S. and other countries were spending billions of dollars on health research to fight infectious disease and improve human health in America and around the world, while these "Defenders of the Faith" were making a perverted mockery out of medical science. The Biological Weapons Treaty, signed in 1973 by 113 nations, demonstrated the world's commitment to a total ban on biological warfare. However the terrorists played by their own rules.

That was one reason Rawlins had fought so hard to become a member of the Biotechnology Export Control Committee. If he couldn't stop naive academicians from training future genetic terrorists, he could at least deny the assholes the tools to carry out their work efficiently. That would leave them ironically overqualified, having effectively been out of action for four or five years pursuing an education they could never apply.

"They'll probably all end up slinging Slurpees at some 7-11," he thought, recalling the many times he had endured the surly behavior of some Middle-Eastern convenience store clerk in Washington. *He'd often wondered about those guys...*

Chapter 5

““Zack!” I’m so glad you’re back, Honey,” said Sally Rawlins to the tired voice on the telephone.

“I’m afraid I have to swing by General Carter’s office first and drop off some stuff. I’ll see you in about an hour, OK? How are the kids?”

“Oh, all right, I guess,” sighed Sally, “Samantha fell down yesterday and split her lip open, and Zack Jr. has refused to do any homework since you left.”

Rawlins always felt guilty about leaving his family for business trips, and perhaps that was why he spent a small fortune each time in the airport duty-free shops. It was shameless bribery but it made him feel better.

“So tell me, Colonel,” demanded the General as Rawlins stepped into his office, “who did it and how?”

Rawlins, accustomed to the DCI’s bluntness, responded without hesitation, “Shomar thinks it was a terrorist group called Fath, and Lab Five thinks they used a weaponized ***E. coli.***”

“Thinks?” growled Carter, “Is that the best you can do, Colonel?”

“Well, Sir, the isolate they found at the Kibbutz was a laboratory strain of bacteria alright, but hardly one that would cause any serious illness, and it contained no FOGs.” Foreign Offensive Genes, or FOGs, included a set of eighteen genes compiled by the U.S. Army Biological Warfare Defense group at Ft. Detrick, Maryland. These genes, from a variety of bacterial sources, encoded some of the most potent toxins known to man and could presumably be engineered into “harmless” bacteria to transform them into killers. Because of this, ultrasensitive DNA probes had been developed at Detrick to detect all eighteen FOGs, and these probes had been shared with Lab Five as part of the Israeli-American Biological Defense Pact. It was this set of probes that had revealed nothing "FOGgy" about the Tafiz isolate.

"Regarding the Fath group," continued Rawlins, "it's only one of seven groups claiming credit, and there's no conclusive evidence yet linking any of them to the attack."

"Well that's just great," said Carter sarcastically. "A biological weapon that couldn't hurt a flea, and a list of seven wild guesses for suspects. We're back to square one."

"No, Sir, not exactly," replied Rawlins. "Lab Five sequenced the isolate and it's a mutant strain. No FOGs that we can identify, but I've asked Dan Reynolds at Cal-Tech to model it. Can we get a secure courier to fly the sequence data out to California right away?"

"No sweat," said the DCI, punching one of twenty buttons on a panel beside his desk.

In seconds, an eager young Lieutenant popped in through the door. "Yes, Sir?"

"Take this disk and this letter from Colonel Rawlins and hand-deliver it, *Code One*, to Dr. Dan Reynolds in the Molecular Modeling Group at Cal-Tech. I want you on the next plane out, and call me from Dr. Reynolds' lab after you have delivered it. That is all."

"Yes, Sir," answered the aide, as he clutched the delivery and popped back out the door.

"Also," resumed Rawlins, "I remembered seeing some HUMINT from M-5 about a year ago that mentioned a group called Fath. The report suggested that they had an interest in Biotechnology. I'm concerned that their strategists might have realized how easy genetic engineering is, and decided to build themselves a poor man's nuclear bomb."

"Get serious, Zack," scoffed the General. "Do you really think a bunch of fundamentalist screwballs could produce BW agents themselves?"

"Crissakes, General," reacted Rawlins, "they sell gene cloning kits at Toys 'R Us!"

"Calm down, Colonel." warned Carter. "Granted, it's a possibility, but in a year? They'd have had to have had Multiplex technology."

A wave of anxiety flooded over Rawlins. Multiplex technology in the hands of terrorists. What a nightmare. That was precisely the reason it was on the Controlled Technology List. Fortunately, he had been successful in restricting Multiplex to the U.S., Japan and Great Britain, so he had eliminated that possibility. *Or had he...?*

As if reading Zack's mind, General Carter ordered, "Call Fred Savage in Export Control, and get a hold of the guys in the Commerce Department and the DIA. I want a list of every organization that purchased a Multiplex system in the last year as well as anyone who bought any part of the system, even the uncontrolled components. I also want positive confirmation where every piece of that equipment is right now."

"Sally, I'm afraid I'm going to be a little longer," apologized Zack over the phone. "I'll try to be home as quick as I can."

"It's OK, Zack, I understand. I'll keep your dinner in the oven."

"Damn," he cursed to himself as he hung up, "she doesn't deserve this." If only he could explain to her how many lives might depend on this—but what would that accomplish? So as usual, the Army was triumphant. *One day I'm just gonna chuck the whole thing...*Then, as abruptly as hanging up the phone, it was gone. His concern for Sally, his guilt over their fading relationship, gone. He'd make it up to her, as soon as he completed his mission. She'd just have to understand.

By the next afternoon, Rawlins had gathered all the available export tracking information in a thick printout on his desk. The complete systems were easy. Ten had gone to universities and companies in the U.K., and seven had been bought by Japan. Individual components however, were another matter. Although his arguments had convinced Congress that complete Multiplex systems, in the wrong hands, could pose a threat to national security, he had been unable to win any restrictions on the sale of individual components, except for the Femtosecond Signal Processor. Unex Corporation, the manufacturer of the hardware, had mobilized a team of lawyers who skillfully and meticulously documented that with the exception of the FSP, all components could potentially be integrated into other technologies. Therefore restricting the distribution of their components put them at a market disadvantage for a broad range of laboratory applications. Moreover, they argued, copycat components would quickly become available from competitors in Taiwan or South Korea, should export controls be imposed.

Fred Savage's people in Export Control had done a superb job, on short notice, of tracking over 200 individual components. Two robotic dilutors to Vitragen in Barcelona, a laser gel-reader to the University of Uppsala in Sweden, even some parts to a company in South Africa.

"South Africa." Zack wondered out loud. "How did they get away with that?" This was getting him nowhere.

Fortunately, a disk had accompanied the hard copy he was examining, so Rawlins quickly slid it into his Pentium III and began sorting. In minutes he had identified all components that had gone to any country that was considered to sponsor terrorism, as well as any country not allied with the U.S. Again, it was more or less a random scattering of sales. Frustrated, Zack reached to clear the file but stopped.

"Just a quick look at sales to friendlies," he murmured.

The chronological list of sales showed nothing of note, but when he grouped them by client, something peculiar stood out. Over a period of four months NewFarma, a large pharmaceuticals company based in London, had purchased a striking number of Multiplex components. The parts had been purchased purportedly for a range of applications within various NewFarma subsidiaries. Once the components were delivered to the parent company however, subsequent distribution was internal, and impossible to track. The disconcerting thing, Rawlins observed, was that if you put all those parts in one room, and added a FSP, you had a complete Multiplex system.

"Jean," called Rawlins over his intercom, "could you get me Nelson Medway in London, please?" Glancing at his watch, he quickly added, "I'm afraid we'll have to bother him at home."

Three minutes later the secretary's voice came over the intercom, "Mr. Medway on line three, Colonel."

"Nelson, its been a long time," said Rawlins. "I'm terribly sorry to call you at home. How have you been?"

"Fine, Zack," came the familiar British accent. "What a surprise to hear from you."

"Is that lovely woman still putting up with you?" kidded Rawlins.

"Millie…?" replied Medway.

"No, the Queen," as both men shared a good laugh. Zack figured his friend was probably on his fifth or sixth glass of sherry by this time of evening.

"Actually," continued Medway, "Millie's away for a while."

"And how about that boy of yours?" asked Rawlins. "Teddy got that Oxford Ph.D. yet?"

For a moment Zack thought they had been cut off, as there was no reply from Medway.

"Teddy was killed last year, about a month before he would have finished at Oxford," came the somber reply.

"Oh, Nelson, I'm so sorry. I had no idea."

Zack didn't ask, but Medway continued, "Teddy was returning home from the library one evening and someone shot him. So far the police have been unable to come up with a suspect. For a while they were looking for an acquaintance of his, some Lebanese graduate student who had been seen with him earlier that evening, but she seems to have just disappeared. I've got some of my friends at Interpol looking for her, but so far all leads seem to dead end at different places in the Middle East. They also have established no motive for the murder. Apparently the only thing missing was his briefcase, but it contained only his research data, no money or valuables. For a while I had an idea that it might have been one of those falsetto screamers who opposed me so violently over making public those Nazi records."

"Nazi records?" asked Rawlins.

"Yes, I had arranged for Teddy to be allowed to study World War II medical records of human experimentation done on POWs by Nazi scientists. Shortly before he was killed, Teddy called to tell me that he had made an important discovery—something about a unique genetic susceptibility among Jews to some type of infection. He also told me that he had decided the data revealed private ethnic information that should not be in the public domain, and he was considering destroying his data and stopping the study. He hadn't published any of his findings up to that point and as far as I know, had only discussed it with me. So I can't imagine he would have made any enemies. I just don't understand it, and I'm afraid Millie hasn't taken it very well. She's been staying with her sister in Edinburgh since the funeral."

"But tell me, Zack," continued Medway, "what can I do for you? I'm certainly glad to hear from you, but this obviously is more than just a social call."

"Well, yes," Rawlins hesitated, "but under the circumstances perhaps I..."

"Nonsense. It's been nearly a year, and I've gotten on with my life. But don't misunderstand me, Zack, I've had to. If I ever find the bastard who killed Teddy, I'll gut him and hang his carcass over Piccadilly Circus. In fact, I'm expecting a call this evening from an Interpol agent who may have some recent information on that student we want to question. How can I help you?"

"Well I wanted to ask if you were still chairman of GENHAZ."

"Why yes, in fact the committee met just last week." GENHAZ, the British Royal Committee on Genetic Hazards, was a mixed group of scientists and politicians formed to monitor scientific and technological advances in genetic engineering that could potentially create risks to people or the environment.

"What do you know about NewFarma?" asked Rawlins.

"NewFarma. Yes, of course. That's a multinational pharmaceuticals company based here in London. Real big on Biotechnology, and bloody secretive about their research projects. Even their purchasing and distribution systems are proprietary. Our committee receives this quarterly confection from them they call their "Science Update," but I'm pretty sure we don't know the half of what they're actually doing."

"What would you say if I told you NewFarma has acquired Multiplex capability?"

"Multiplex! Come on, old boy. We may not be Scotland Yard, but GENHAZ knows where every Multiplex system is in the U.K."

"What about a system that was assembled over several months, from a series of purchases of individual components? Our records show that NewFarma has purchased enough components to build a Multiplex, except for the FSP."

"But even if that were their intention," countered Medway, "without the chip its just so much gadgetry."

"I understand that but still, is there any way you could look into NewFarma and see what they did with all those components?"

"I'm afraid that may be a bit of a sticky-wicket Zack, but certainly, we'll have a go at it."

"Carter."

"Good afternoon, General. Colonel Rawlins. I wanted to let you know what we've come up with on tracking Multiplex components. All the complete systems have been legitimately purchased by responsible organizations, and there does not appear to be anything unusual about sales of individual components except for one company. NewFarma in London, over the last four months, has bought all the components of a complete system except for the FSP. Now that's not necessarily anything to be concerned about, but I'm checking it out."

"A complete system except for the FSP?" interrupted the DCI. "Any chance of them getting the chip?"

"I don't see how. Not without our knowing, at least. I got a hold of Nelson Medway at GENHAZ, for some more information on NewFarma and their current research programs. I'll let you know the moment he gets back to me."

"Nelson Medway on line three, Colonel," called Jean over the intercom.

"Boy, you guys work fast, Nelson," said Rawlins. "What did you find?"

"Something interesting, and a bit surprising," came the reply. "I say, what's this all about anyway, Zack? NewFarma is owned by Neulieb, a holding company based in Switzerland, with branches in several odd locations including Bulgaria and Russia. I think GENHAZ needs to know some more about your interest in this company."

"There's really nothing to tell, Nelson. Our Export Control Committee just turned up this odd grouping of purchases in an audit, and we simply want to be sure everything is legit." Rawlins hated misleading his old friend, but he had a big enough public relations problem already. Congressmen who were supported by the Biotech industry regularly had him on the carpet on Capitol Hill, and his committee was constantly embroiled in litigation. Then there were organizations like Britain's Dangerous Pathogens Monitoring Group, and the Green Party in Germany, who would give anything to accuse Rawlins and the United States of approving the sale of equipment used in Bio-War research.

"There's something else, Zack," added Medway. "We had a peculiar incident here about six months ago. I remember it because it was shortly before Teddy's death. I didn't think much of it until your call, but now I think you should know about it. Unex Corporation received an emergency service call from the Molecular Genetics lab at Oxford, which as you know had some time before purchased a complete Multiplex system. The caller claimed the Femtosecond Signal Processor had failed and their system was down. As this was a priority warranty repair, Unex sent a technician out from New York with a new chip right away. It seems their representative made it to Heathrow, but then he just disappeared. When Unex called Oxford, after hearing nothing from their technician in several days, no one in the lab had seen him and what's more, no one knew anything about a repair request. Their system is working and there has never been any problem with the FSP. Police here are treating the case as a simple missing person, but what we also have is a missing FSP chip."

Chapter 6

Sergei Gordaleyev knew they were lying again. Three workers at the Kirishi Agricultural Research Plant and seven members of their families had suddenly become very ill. One child had died. This was not the first time unexplained illness had broken out at the plant and as before, management had issued a statement disclaiming any responsibility. This time they blamed the incident on contaminated drinking water in the town and accused sanitation workers of improper maintenance procedures. The guilty technician, they said, had confessed to his negligence and had been sent to a work camp in Siberia. Also as before, management held to the position that the plant was engaged exclusively in the development of new and better varieties of agricultural products, and new biological controls for agricultural pests.

Sergei was not a scientist, but he was a conscientious and observant worker. In his seven years as a fermentation technician at the Kirishi plant he had seen too many safety violations and far too many injuries. When he reported these problems to his supervisors he found their explanations unsatisfactory, and their promises of change were never carried out. Frustrated and angry, Sergei finally took his complaints to the *Minmedbioprom*, the Ministry of the Medical and Microbiological Industry, in nearby St. Petersburg. This office was responsible for the management of industrial biotechnology in Russia. An assistant safety officer listened carefully as Sergei related years of safety violations, injuries and cover-ups, and promised to take action immediately. This turned out to be the only promise his superiors ever kept, as two days later he was called in before the deputy plant manager and summarily dismissed from his job.

Now two years later, Sergei cleaned the streets of Kirishi and greeted many of his former co-workers as they passed by each morning on the two mile walk out of town to the plant. Although still his friends, they were tight-lipped about conditions at the plant. Only his friend since childhood, Boris Dutrev, would share any information, and then only late at night in the safety of Sergei's one-room flat.

"I tell you, Sergei," said Boris one evening after several glasses of vodka, "I am worried. You know the new Molecular Biology Institute they were just completing when you left? Well, rumors are flying about what they do in there."

"Rumors?" asked Sergei. "What kind of rumors?"

"Well first of all, security at the plant has increased tremendously. You of course have seen the new, three-meter-high fence topped with barbed wire around the entire plant. Around the Institute itself there is now an additional double fence, with fierce dogs running loose between the two lines. There is only one entrance through the fence and the gate is guarded twenty-four hours by Red Army soldiers carrying Kalashnikovs. Kalashnikovs! To guard an agricultural research facility?"

"So what do you make of it, old friend?"

"Sergei," answered Boris, his voice quavering, "I think the Institute is being used to make biological weapons."

The two men stared at each other. Simultaneously denying and believing the idea, their confusion held them mute. Finally it was Sergei who spoke.

"We must get this out through the *Samizdat.*" Samizdat was an underground system of printing and distributing illegal and dissident literature in the Russia, and Sergei had become active in the system after his dismissal from the Kirishi plant.

"If we are caught we will surely go to prison, or worse," protested Boris.

"Do no worry, I will do this myself. There will be no way you can be connected with this information. Besides, comrade, are we not in the era of *Glasnost*?" Under other circumstances the sarcasm of Sergei's remark would have made both men laugh, but the issue was far too serious.

"Dr. Reynolds, I think you should see this," called the excited voice from the darkness of the graphics display room.

"I'll be right there, Tim," answered the Professor.

Tim Scully was the star graduate student in Dan Reynolds' stable at Cal Tech. The consummate computer geek, he could have been sent over from Central Casting. Thick glasses, unkempt hair and a thin, scraggly beard disguised pure brilliance. For Tim, the learning curve had lasted only about six months into his graduate program. From that point on he began re-writing the book on molecular graphics. By the end of his second year he had designed and patented a totally new approach to graphics design that would soon make both him and Cal Tech quite wealthy. Multifactorial Iterative Structure Integration, or "Missy," as they affectionately called it, was a modeling program that used Artificial Intelligence to simultaneously change up to ten features of the structure of a molecule. As a change to any one feature affected the other nine features, for a single run Missy had to analyze over a million possible structures. The system "learned" by pruning out the least likely results in each cycle. In this way the program was quickly able to predict the most probable conformation of the molecule that would result from the changes. With a special kinetics subroutine he had written for Missy, Tim was further able to predict the effects such changes in structure would have on the function of the molecule. Thus the problem Colonel Rawlins' courier delivered to Dr. Reynolds was tailor-made for Missy.

"The structure on the left represents the normal *E. coli* toxin molecule," said Tim, pointing to the split-screen display. "On the right is Missy's predicted structure for the mutated toxin."

"Not much difference, is there?" noted Reynolds.

"Not much. Just a little hump here at Alanine 162 and a slightly deeper cleft at the active site. But watch when I insert acetylcholinesterase, the toxin's target molecule, and turn on kinetics."

On the left screen both watched as a stream of target molecules entered the display and encountered the normal toxin. About every tenth molecule appeared to catch on the toxin and swing into position at the active site. The target then began to bulge and distort, atomic bonds strained to their limit, and then simply disintegrated. In contrast, the right hand screen was an uninterrupted blur of activity.

"I'll slow down the activity of the mutant toxin," said Scully as he typed in a command. Target molecules were now entering both displays at the same rate, but virtually every one that encountered the mutant toxin was destroyed.

"Almost 100% efficiency," declared Reynolds.

"And don't forget," added his student, "we're running the mutant's kinetics at one-one thousandth actual speed."

Scully turned from the screen and looked up at his mentor. The results were astounding. The gene sequence from Colonel Rawlins encoded a mutant toxin that was ten thousand times more active than its normal counterpart. That made it easily the most powerful, and dangerous toxin known.

"Zack," came the excited voice over the telephone, "Dan Reynolds. Tim and I just finished modeling your gene sequence. Boy, you've got a hot one on your hands. I can't tell you why the bacteria are resistant to antibiotics, but I can sure tell you why your patient is sick. That poor soul has got a toxigenic strain of *E. coli* that is far more dangerous than anything I've heard of. Even botulism toxin is tame compared to the stuff this bug puts out. You better tell your clinician friends that whatever they do, don't let that one get out of isolation."

"Thanks, Dan, will do. I knew I could count on you. You've really done an outstanding job with this one. If you can have the data on disk within an hour, I'll call Norton Air Force Base and get a courier over to pick it up, along with my original data disk."

"No sweat. If you like, I can FAX a hard copy immediately," offered Reynolds.

"No, don't do that," Rawlins reacted, and then quickly added, "I mean, I just don't want to risk the wrong person seeing this information and getting all excited unnecessarily. You understand. After you make the disk copy, please erase the file from the Cray, and I'd appreciate it if you wouldn't discuss this with anyone for the time being."

"Whatever you say, Zack. What's the big secret anyway? The patient is in isolation isn't he?"

"Yes, of course, but you know how the media can get carried away with something like this."

"Please come in, Mr. Medway," said the Director of Public Relations. "Welcome to NewFarma. It's an honor meeting you, Sir. Would you care for some tea?"

"No, thank you, Mr. Vincent."

"Mark, Mark Vincent. Please, sit down. So tell me, to what do we owe the honor of this visit from the chairman of GENHAZ?"

"I'll get right to the point, Mr. Vincent."

"Mark, please call me Mark."

"Very well, Mark. GENHAZ has reason to believe that NewFarma has acquired a Multiplex DNA sequencing system. We wish to verify this and if it is true, we need to see a protocol for its use and planned applications."

The Director was caught a little off guard by Medway's bluntness, and he stalled, "A Multiplex what?"

"DNA sequencer," replied Medway. "What are your company's planned applications for this system?"

Vincent had by now regained his composure. "Actually, Mr. Medway, I believe there must be some mistake. I am not aware of any such equipment at NewFarma, but if you would like to wait a moment, we can have a look at the major equipment acquisitions file." Entering a command on his computer keyboard, the Director brought up the supply system program.

Medway feigned indifference over Vincent's preliminary search operations, while concentrating discreetly on the keyboard as the invisible secret access code was entered. H-O-N-E-S-T-Y. *Honesty! Charming,* thought Medway. As Vincent scrolled rapidly through the last year's major purchases, Medway saw several Multiplex components pass by. He said nothing, but noted that they all displayed a number three in the destination code column.

"There," stated Vincent as he reached the end of the file. "No Multiplex system. It is of course New Farma policy to comply with all GENHAZ reporting requirements, but I just wanted to reassure myself as well as you that there had not been some sort of slip-up."

"We appreciate that, Mark," replied Medway. "I'm sorry to have troubled you."

"Absolutely no trouble at all." Vincent smiled professionally as he extended his hand to Medway, whose thoughts were already organizing a plan to break into NewFarma's supply database.

"Dr. Reynolds!" blurted out Tim Scully as he burst into the professor's office. "We've lost main memory on the Cray!"

"Lost it?"

"Yeah—gone! All data, all software, even all systems programs. Its just wiped out. I was sitting there, doing some routine sorting, and the screen went blank. I tried to call up several programs, but no luck. It won't even accept a re-boot. I don't know what happened, but something really nuked our system."

"This is Colonel Rawlins, General. I just received the analysis back from Dan Reynolds and I'd like to discuss it with you as soon as possible."

"Fine. You can come up right now."

Five minutes later Rawlins was in General Carter's office.

"Looks like Lab Five may be right about a weaponized *E. coli*, General. The structural changes in this mutant strain are minor, almost inapparent, but the effects on the function of the toxin are unbelievable. Whoever engineered this bug really knew what they were doing."

"And really worked fast," added the General.

Both men knew what that remark meant. With standard molecular biology laboratory equipment, determining the DNA sequence of the *E. coli*, designing and installing mutations in particular genes, and verifying the construction would take years. On top of that, targeting a particular molecule with any precision within a human population would require additional years of work on the target DNA sequence.

Every sphincter in Rawlins' body tightened as he slowly stated the obvious. "Some sonofabitch out there has a Multiplex and they're using it for BW."

The general asked, "Have you heard any more from…"

As if on cue the intercom interrupted him. "Nelson Medway on four, General."

"Mr. Medway. Perfect timing! I was just going to call you. Zack Rawlins is here with me now. I'll put you on the speaker so you can give us both the scoop. Have you found out anything more about NewFarma and its purchases of Multiplex components?"

"Yes, General. In fact I have some rather disconcerting news. I'm afraid I can't tell you how I obtained this information, but most if not all of the components purchased by NewFarma in London were delivered to the Kirishi Agricultural Research Laboratory in Russia. Zack, old friend, I think its time for straight talk on this."

Rawlins turned to General Carter, who nodded.

"I'll be in London tomorrow morning, Nelson."

Chapter 7

"Have a look at this," said Geoffrey Fitzsimmons as he handed his superior the latest HUMINT transmission from M-5's agent in St. Petersburg. "Samizdat is urging Russian citizens to demand an investigation into the recent outbreak of illness in Kirishi. They believe the problem is related to some type of industrial waste from the Agricultural Research Institute. They also want an explanation for the new added security measures at the plant."

"Sounds like they're after Kostyakova again," replied the Section Chief. Cheslav Kostyakova, the head of Minmedbioprom, was the former First Secretary of the Kirishi *Gorkom*, the City Party Committee, and a rising star in Russian politics. Prior to those positions he had served as the director of the Kirishi Institute, where he had introduced biotechnology to Russia through the Single Cell Protein project. During his tenure in Kirishi he had endured increasingly vocal attacks from Russian environmentalists who claimed that SCP production was polluting nearby Lake Ladoga and causing serious allergic reactions among the residents of Kirishi. Kostyakova responded to these charges by increasing security at the Institute dramatically, virtually eliminating public access to information about plant operations. He also coerced local party officials in Kirishi into quelling public protests against pollution from the factory. When a mysterious epidemic began among plant workers and spread to the town, killing scores of children and older people, the news was so effectively suppressed that the region's sanitary and epidemiological station in nearby St.

Petersburg was never officially informed. It was only through Samizdat that the information was ever leaked.

"Did you note the last line?" asked Fitzsimmons. "They want a public declaration from Minmedbioprom that none of the research being conducted at Kirishi is in violation of the 1973 Geneva treaty banning biological weapons. What do you make of that?"

"Frankly," replied Section Chief Barrett, "it sounds like very clever KGB disinformation."

"You aren't serious," said Fitzsimmons, "are you?"

"Why not? Do you realize how much intelligence effort NATO will pour into this if they suspect Kirishi is a BW facility? Particularly those American blokes—they'll reposition satellites, pull agents from other assignments and be all over us here at M-5 to do the same."

"Are you saying you aren't going to release this? What about the MOU on Russian HUMINT?"

"Oh, I'll release it—a sanitized version. Just leave out the last line."

Fitzsimmons had always trusted Barrett's judgement, but he had a bad feeling about this one.

"Zack! So good to see you," said Medway. "Come in, come in. Please sit down. May I get you some tea or coffee?"

"No, thanks, Nelson, I had plenty on the plane. I want to thank you for all the help you've been on this NewFarma case, and apologize for not being more up front with you about the entire situation. Frankly, we've got a real problem here. A short time ago, an Israeli settlement on the West Bank was wiped out by a terrorist attack. The attack was frighteningly effective, and the Israelis have released no official information yet to the press. They believe it was BW, employing a weaponized *E. coli*. Shomar asked us for help but when I investigated, things didn't add up. The bug that was isolated at the site was a mutant alright, but to engineer such a mutation would have required technology that simply isn't available to any terrorist group."

"The Multiplex NewFarma delivered to Kirishi..." said Medway, as both men paused to consider the unthinkable.

"We have no proof, of course," continued Rawlins, "but I feel it would be unwise to discount the possibility. Did you ever locate that missing FSP chip?"

"I'm afraid not."

"Then I'm afraid we'll have to assume the worst. Can you check with M-5 and see what they have on Kirishi? I'm particularly interested in anything they've got on the Molecular Biology Institute there. There's one more thing I'd like to ask of you, Nelson, and please just tell me if you would rather not. Would it be possible for me to get a look at Teddy's research notes?"

"Certainly, Zack. I collected all the papers from Teddy's flat, and I have them in a box in the back office. Really not much, I'm afraid, but you are welcome to look through them."

Teddy Medway's notes were pretty much in random order, heaped into a large box along with some books, other coursework and miscellaneous papers. Sorting through the mess, Rawlins noticed a handwritten reminder about a teaching assistants' meeting, addressed to a Nayah Salim.

"Nelson," called Rawlins as he stepped out of the small back office, "did the police ever locate that classmate of Teddy's who was with him the night he died?"

"What? His classmate? No, they are still looking for her, but as I told you, her trail stops in the Middle East. Why?"

"Was the name Salim—Nayah Salim?"

"Salim. Let me see. Yes, that was her name."

"Did Teddy ever talk about her? What sort of research did she do?"

"She was a molecular biologist, and an excellent one, according to Teddy. In fact he was most impressed with her. He once said she could clone anything. She's also the best lead we have, in finding Teddy's murderer, and I'm determined to track her down. But what's all this got to do with NewFarma, and Kirishi?"

"Perhaps nothing. I don`t know. There's really not much of any use here in Teddy's notes," sighed Rawlins.

"I was afraid you would be disappointed. He always kept his findings in his briefcase. He never let it out of his sight."

As Rawlins neared the bottom of the box an abbreviation on one of the pages caught his attention. ACH—acetylcholinesterase. That was the target molecule of the toxin produced by the isolate from Tafiz kibbutz. Concentrating on the scribblings, Rawlins confirmed what he had suspected. Teddy had uncovered what appeared to be a genetic hypersensitivity among Jews to the effects of a bacterial toxin. If the information were accurate, it revealed an "Achilles heel" in much of the Israeli population.

"Should we send this one up to Rawlins' office?" Jeff Cunningham asked his boss.

Roger Beck took a cursory glance at the transmission. "Yeah, I guess. It doesn't look like much, but they said they wanted to see anything about disease outbreaks or biomedical research in Russia. Just send it up in the guard mail." Beck paused, and then added, "No, wait. Kirishi Agricultural Research Institute? I tell you what, Jeff, let's just sit on this one and see if we get a follow-up."

The two men screened all intelligence transmissions on the Russians that were forwarded to the CIA by M-5. The MOU between the two intelligence organizations was, in principle, an excellent idea. However at times Beck wondered whose side the Brits were actually on. More times than the analyst cared to remember, M-5's "intelligence" reports had turned out to be nothing more than petulant complaints from disgruntled local Russian officials, or worse, purposeful KGB disinformation. In fact he had been burned so many times by this problem that he had long ago ceased going to General Quarters over every "hot tip" from M-5.

As usual, it was the middle of the night when the heavy knock came at the door.

"Comrade Dutrev, open the door. We wish to speak to you."

Aroused from sleep, Boris hurried awkwardly to the door. "Yes?" he asked timidly of the two men awaiting him.

"Put on your coat. You are coming with us."

The late night arrests were a clever tactic. There were seldom any witnesses, and the sleepy victims were usually confused and quite vulnerable.

"Mr. Medway? I'm Geoffrey Fitzsimmons from M-5, CBW defense section. I saw your inquiry to us about the Kirishi Agricultural Institute."

"Oh yes, please, come in. Quite good of you for responding so quickly, but you really didn't have to come over here yourself. I would have..."

"Actually," the younger man interrupted, "I'm doing this on my own. Section Chief Barrett doesn't know I've come and I'm afraid there would be hell to pay if he did."

"Oh...?" said Medway.

"Yes. You see, we recently received a transmission from our agent in St. Petersburg regarding the Institute in Kirishi. The report concerned a suspicious disease outbreak in the town. In fact we already forwarded the information to the chaps at the CIA, that is, most of the information. My boss felt parts of the report represented disinformation, so he had me sanitize it first. I just did as I was directed and said nothing, until I saw the GENHAZ request for information."

"So what was it you deleted from the report?"

"Samizdat is urging citizens to demand that Minmedbioprom publicly certify that the Kirishi is not conducting BW research."

Chapter 8

"Its a virus," declared Scully, "and the most virulent one I've ever seen."

"What about our vaccine program?" said Reynolds. "Nothing's ever gotten by that before. Even the Memorial Day virus that practically shut down the Defense Department couldn't touch us."

"Well I'd like to meet the person who designed this one. I'd tell him it was nothing short of genius—that is, before I kicked his ass. I've checked all our inputs. The only way the virus could have entered our system was on that disk from Colonel Rawlins. He better have his people take a look at the disk we sent him, before they get it like we did. Its going to take me weeks to bring the Cray back on line."

Above the loud hum of the main machine room, Dov Messer's excited voice caused all heads to turn. "What the hell? Is someone running an unauthorized test? What's happened to main memory?"

Moments later the system died, and the machine room fell into eerie silence. Then, as if to mock them, the irritating buzz of the system failure alarm cut in. The technicians at the main console frantically punched in their recovery routines, but without effect. Within seconds telephone modems began ringing as operators from the remote stations, unaware that the main system had crashed, tried vainly to re-establish communications.

When Dov Messer had proposed consolidating all military intelligence communications under Lab Five's computer system, the vastly increased efficiency and speed of the new system carried broad appeal. Minister Shoram, looking for ways to absorb the effects of a slowdown in defense-related American foreign aid, welcomed the substantial cost savings of the idea and the plan was implemented. Messer's reputation as a computer system expert was so highly respected that no one dared to ask what might happen if the main system suffered an irrecoverable failure. So now Israel stood naked to attack, with over 90 percent of its military communications system knocked out.

"Zack? Dan Reynolds. I'm glad I got you. Have you received the disk from us yet?"

"Yes, thanks a lot Dan. We..."

"Don't load it! Have you loaded it yet?"

"Yes, I just had it copied into our main system. Why? Is there a problem?"

"Have you got a disinfectant program?"

"Disinfectant? I...yes, of course. What's going on?"

"Shut down all your modems and external communications, and run your disinfectant program. I think you've got a red hot virus on your hands. Call me back when you're done. Just do it!"

"Answer the phone, dammit," cursed Rawlins. "Where is everybody?" In the control suite of the Pentagon's massive underground computer operations center the telephone rang unheeded, lost in the cacophony of alarms. Captain Sheila White, the Command Duty Officer, shouted orders at the operators, as system after system locked up and crashed. By the time the express elevator released Rawlins into the sub-basement it was all over. The anger and frustration in the face of Captain White, and the shrill alarms blaring in the dead silence of the machine room told the story.

"I'm sorry, Colonel," said Captain White, "I tried to stop it. It happened so fast."

"Never mind, Captain. What external comm lines do you have open?"

"We're on line to the DIA and the National Security Agency at Ft. Meade, oh, and NASA."

"NASA? Shit! Get some people on the phones. Call all those agencies. Tell them to shut down their systems and run their best viral disinfectant program."

"Yes, Sir," replied the Captain as she relayed the orders to her operators.

"Captain White," called one of the operators moments later, "Ft. Meade just called. The NSA system crashed."

"DIA, too," called a second operator.

"Anybody get through to NASA yet?" said Captain White.

"Yes, Ma'am," came the answer. "I think we just got 'em in time. They shut their system down as directed, but the supervisor's super-pissed and wants to know what the hell's going on."

Turning to Rawlins, the Captain's eyes relayed the request.

"It looks like I allowed some sort of super virus to infect our system," explained the Colonel. "I take full responsibility for it. Double check for any other users we may have infected, then give me a damage report ASAP."

"Mr. Messer to see you, Minister."

"Send him in."

The door opened and Dov Messer hurried in.

"Dov, what the hell happened? Do you realize the situation we are in? No military data communications at all, to anyplace! You told me this system could not crash—it was failsafe."

"Minister Shoram, it appears to be some kind of virus. I..."

"I don't want excuses, Dov. I want our communications system up, and I want it up now! We'll get to the cause of this later. Do you understand me?"

"Yes, Sir," replied Messer. "We're tearing the CPU apart now. We'll have an answer within a couple of hours."

"Hours!" roared the DM. "Are you listening to me, Dov? I'm talking minutes! I want that system up immediately. Do you realize the defensive position this puts us in? What if the Syrians find out we're crippled? We are swimming in a sea of sharks here, and your system failure has just poured a bucket of blood into the water."

"It is done," said Ibn Nimer as he looked up from the handwritten message. "Allah be praised. The Zionists' computer system is destroyed. Send the message to Kamil. Commence *Operation Majdi.*"

The stifling heat made Kamil irritable as he waited impatiently for further orders. It was now more than a fortnight since he had been directed to wait in the one room flat in Kiryat, a small Israeli town near the Syrian border. Details of the mission, he was told, would come soon by courier, along with further instructions about the weapon now sitting in a box in the flat's small refrigerator. When electrical power went off for several hours, he had considered contacting his superiors for instructions on what to do about the weapon. However he remembered the orders he was given, to communicate with no one.

"What kind of a weapon needs to be in a refrigerator?" he thought. "Who needs these mystery devices. Just give me fifty kilos of high explosives and a detonator—I will strike a blow they will never forget." Kamil was uneducated, the son of a Bedouin, but his heritage made him the Arab's Arab. The Bedouin is a man with stars for a roof, and his fierce independence made him popular and well respected among the Fath leadership. Orphaned at the age of thirteen, he had come to Jerusalem to find work, where he was quickly caught up in the excitement of the resistance movement. To a young boy it was but a surrealistic game. Kamil and his friends would pelt the Israeli soldiers with rocks, and then scatter down the twisting, narrow alleys as the troops gave chase. The game ended cruelly one day when his friend Hamal, rising from behind a wall to launch another rock, pitched violently backward on top of him, his brain shattered by a bullet. From that instant on, Kamil's life was committed. There would be no negotiations, there would be no compromise.

"It's worse than I thought," said Scully, as he and Reynolds examined the circuit board under the dual-headed microscope. "This board's riddled with micro burn-outs."

"The virus must have initiated thousand of infinite 'do-loops' at discrete locations, causing highly focused overheating," theorized Reynolds. "We may have to replace every board in the system."

"This sure wasn't just some bored hacker's prank," said Scully. "Someone wanted to take out our system, big time, and they sure knew how to do it."

"Dan? Zack. Judging by what just happened here, and your phone call, I'd guess you've had some big problems with your system."

"That's putting it mildly, Zack. A virus got past our vaccine program and took out the Cray. We're pretty sure it came in on your disk, and probably hitched a ride back to you on our disk, in an active form, along with the modeling data. Were you able to disinfect in time?"

"I'm afraid not. We got clobbered, along with DIA and NSA, who were on line with us at the time. Fortunately NASA shut down in time, or the entire U.S. space program might be out of business now."

"Where did that damn disk come from, anyway?" demanded Reynolds.

"One of our allies, Dan, but I'm sorry I can't tell you any more now. I'm going to try to get to the bottom of this and I'll let you know as soon as I find out anything that may help you."

"I don't think there's a whole lot anyone can do at this point, Zack. Have you checked out any of your main boards? This thing actually hit the ***hardware***. I've never heard of anything like that."

"Dov," said Ana Weisner, the day shift supervisor, "this doesn't make sense. All of our system inputs are vaccinated, plus at the moment the virus hit we had no transmissions in progress. I checked the operations record. I also inspected all disks that we received and imported into the system over the last week and they are all virus-free."

"So what are you saying?" Messer asked suspiciously.

"I think we were infected by someone from inside Lab Five."

"Do you realize what you are saying? Who have you told of this?"

"No one, Dov, just you, but I think we better let Minister Shoram know immediately."

"Yes, of course. I'll go to him personally. Meanwhile, tell no one about this. Is that clear?"

The inspection port for the pump was on the south side of the pump housing, two meters above the ground, just where the instructions said it would be. Kamil quickly unfastened the bolts on the cover with a small crescent wrench, and rotated the plate to one side. Pulling the metal container from his pocket he opened the lid and extracted the small glass vial. With a sharp twist he broke the top off of the vial at the pre-scored neck and dropped both pieces into the sump.

"*Allahuakhbar*," he breathed, as he slid the cover back into place and bolted it down. Kamil worked nervously, feeling very exposed under the bright illumination of the full moon. The pumping station sat on the crest of a ridge, where it pulled water up from a large aqueduct on one side and propelled it down a ten-inch pipe to a large, open reservoir in the kibbutz on the other side of the valley below. He could not understand the timing of this mission. No Bedouin would plan an attack during a full moon. Although he was respectful of the Fath leadership he was also disdainful of their lack of understanding of the desert. They were city Arabs, which made them a lower order than Bedouins, yet they were his superiors.

Kamil opened the pump control box housing and pushed the purge button, holding it in for a full ten seconds as a rush of water surged through the sump, sweeping its deadly contents up and into the main water line that dropped down the rocky hillside to the lights of the settlement below. He gazed down at the lights, vaguely disappointed that there were no explosions, no screams, in fact no apparent result at all from his actions. *This is no way to fight*, he thought as he fingered the curved sheath of the knife tucked under his waistband.

Chapter 9

"Charlie Bravo Two at Mossat-Bar," Samuels almost shouted as he read the printout curling off his teletype. With his left hand dialing the Prime Minister's office on his secure telephone, his right hand punched the intercom button. "David, alert the ERT. I want you in the air in five minutes. We have another Charlie Bravo Two. This time at Mossat-Bar, up near Syria. Do you have the DNA probes from the Tafiz isolate ready yet?"

"They're coming off the synthesizer today, Major. I'll have them purified and ready for the sensor tomorrow."

"I want the team in full bioprotection level four gear. I'm coming with you on this one."

"Yes, Sir," answered Captain Steinberg. He didn't relish the idea of conducting BW surveys in those awkward spacesuits, particularly in the desert in August, but he understood the danger of going to the scene unprotected.

Looking down as they approached Mossat-Bar, Major Samuels grimly surveyed the settlement. Bodies dotted the rocky compound. As the chopper touched the ground, Samuels hopped out awkwardly in his BC-4 suit. His attention was immediately caught by the still form of a young soldier wearing the uniform of the International Peacekeeping Force. Scanning the area for survivors, the ERT members moved out from the landing zone. Among the nearly fifty residents found dead in the settlement were the bodies of ten members of a Swedish contingent from the International Peacekeeping Force.

"Poor devils," murmured Samuels. "They must have bivouacked here last night. Well there will be no keeping the lid on this now."

Ana Herzog wearily grasped the handle of her overstuffed briefcase and slipped quietly out the door of her flat into the pre-dawn darkness. She was the day shift supervisor of the computer center in Lab Five, and since the system failure nearly two days ago she had slept not more than six hours. For the last two nights she had arrived home long after her husband and two young daughters had gone to sleep, and had left for work in the morning a full two hours before they arose. Her scrutiny of the system operations records appeared to eliminate any outside source for the virus that had infected the system. She reported her suspicions to Dov Messer but to her knowledge, no action was taken. Now she was sure that the virus had originated internally, and she intended to take her findings to the Director.

The green Fiat was parked at the curb in its usual place in front of her building. Her mind dulled by the early hour and lack of sleep, Ana neglected to carry out her morning ritual of checking to see if anyone had tampered with her car. In the instant the starter motor whirred to life she realized her mistake, but it was too late. An orange fireball erupted around her as the explosion catapulted the blazing car across the street.

At Mossat-Bar, Captain Steinberg supervised his medical technicians in obtaining specimens from the victims for analysis. For each body, a large gauge needle and syringe was used for cardiac puncture. Steinberg knew that after death the heart was the only place that could provide a blood sample without cutting open the body, but the procedure still made him feel ghoulish.

"After you have your samples, David, I want the bodies buried in one mass grave," said Major Samuels. "Then decon your team and get them back on the chopper."

The few survivors at the settlement had already been stripped naked and vigorously scrubbed by the ERT, clothed in sterile paper jumpsuits and medevaced out. After a thorough medical examination they would each be carefully questioned by trained epidemiologists to determine what they had done, or not done, that enabled them to survive.

Captain Roald Bjornsen, Officer-in-Charge of the Swedish detachment, appeared visibly shaken at the de-briefing with his Commanding Officer in the International Peacekeeping Force headquarters in Tel Aviv.

"At approximately 1600 hours the patrol's truck had engine trouble, about two kilometers from Mossat-Bar. Their Sergeant radioed to base that they would continue on to the settlement on foot. I directed him to have his patrol set up camp outside of the village, and to interfere as little as possible with the activities of the residents. At 2000 hours the Sergeant radioed that they had established a position and were ready to secure for the night. He reported that he had only contacted the settlers once, to inform them of his patrol's presence and to obtain water. We received a radio check at midnight, and then nothing. When the distress call from the villagers was received this morning we immediately sent a team to Mossat-Bar and found the patrol—dead, every one."

"Any signs of an attack?" asked the Commander.

"No, Sir. None of the troops had any outward sign of injury, and no weapons appeared to have been fired."

"What is the disposition of the bodies?"

"I am sorry, Sir, but I do not know. Shortly after our team arrived at the camp, the Israeli Emergency Reaction Team arrived by helicopter and cordoned off the entire settlement. Our people were directed to leave the area and return to base by the head of the ERT, a Major Samuels. They never actually examined the victims."

"When is Major Samuels going to give us a situation report?"

"All our team leader was told was that a SITREP would be coming down through channels, and that inquiries should be directed to the office of the Minister of Defense."

"Thank you for informing me," said the Defense Minister. "If there is anything I can do, please let me know." The director of computer operations for Lab Five had just called the DM to relay the news of Ana Weisner's death. Shomar was angry and confused. He knew Ana personally, knew her two young daughters by name. Why would terrorists target her? On top of that, Lab Five had lost its day shift supervisor and one of the most conscientious computer technicians in the organization, at an extremely bad time.

"Mrs. Raebel," the DM called into his intercom.

"Yes, Sir?"

"Please have Dov Messer come to my office immediately."

"K-12 strain *E. coli* in every one of the samples," murmured Steinberg as he reviewed the results his technician handed him. Water samples from Mossat-Bar, as well as blood samples from all the victims including the Peacekeeping Force personnel were positive.

"What's wrong with the assay for the toxin gene?" he asked the technician. Although one of their DNA probes had positively identified the presence of K-12 strain *E. coli* in the samples, the specific probe for the mutant toxin gene had yielded inconclusive results.

"I've repeated the assay twice," answered the technician, "but the hybridization is only weakly positive. Its like the probe matches the gene in this isolate, but not 100%. The sample is on the Multiplex now, and I've targeted the toxin gene for sequencing. We should have the data this afternoon."

"Come in Dov, have a seat," said the DM. "You of course know about Ana."

"Yes, Sir, it was quite a shock."

"What about her family?"

"We've taken up a collection for flowers, and one of the wives is watching the children at her house so Ana's husband can make arrangements. She has family in Tel-Aviv, and I understand several of them are at the flat now, doing what they can to help out."

"Well I'm glad things seem to be under control. Dov there's another reason I called you in to see me. I am seriously concerned about the slow recovery of our computer system. I know you are trying hard to bring it back on line, and losing Ana isn't going to make things any easier, but I want you to know just how serious the situation is. This is very sensitive information, and I expect you will discuss it with no one outside this office."

"Of course, Sir."

"A few days ago Israel was attacked with a biological weapon. The target was a remote settlement, and the results were devastating. Now our intelligence people report increased troop activity to the north and east of Israel, as well as the re-positioning of numerous SCUD-B mobile missile batteries. These missiles can be equipped with BW warheads, and I am concerned this may have already been done. With our military communications system down we are virtually at the mercy of our Syrian and Lebanese brothers. I don't think they realize just how crippled our defenses really are but if they did..."

"I understand, Sir. Let me assure you that my staff is putting maximum effort into the system repairs and if I knew a way to do it quicker, I would. The damage is really unbelievable, particularly to the hardware. I must tell you frankly that the loss of our best supervisor is a real setback, but we will get the job done, I promise you."

"Thanks, Dov. We're lucky to have you on the team."

Chapter 10

"Minister Shoram," said General Morah, "the situation is most grave. We have only our secure telephones and teletypes to communicate between bases, and only radio to the outposts. I have been receiving reports of increasing enemy troop movements in southern Syria, and in the Bekaa valley."

"These troop movements. Do you consider them a significant change in threat posture?"

"Yes, Sir, I do. The deployments appear coordinated with the re-positioning of their SCUD-B mobile missile batteries."

"Could those particular SCUDs be equipped with BW warheads?"

"Yes, I believe so. Why?"

"We just had another Charlie Bravo Two, Ben. This time near Syria, in a settlement called Mossat-Bar. Over ninety percent casualties. I'm afraid the terrorists' success with this BW agent might encourage our enemies to try a large scale attack. Are our airfields and storage facilities in the north in range of the SCUDs?"

"Easily," replied Morah.

"What about Tel-Aviv. Could they hit us in the city?"

"I'm afraid so. Particularly from the batteries in the Bekaa. Minister Shoram, I believe we are faced with an imminent threat, and we must take appropriate action for the survival of Israel. Do you not agree?"

"I do," came the reply.

"Nuclear strike?" thundered General Carter. "Did you say threatened, or..."

"Carried out, sir," replied the ashen-faced Lieutenant, "and our satellite just confirmed two bursts in the Bekaa valley of Lebanon."

"Get me Minister Shoram's office ASAP."

"I'll try, Sir, but DOD has clamped a MINIMIZE on all transmissions to the Middle East. Also the Israeli communication network appears to have suffered some sort of major casualty. The only thing that is getting through at all is commercial telephone, and its pretty bad."

"The hell with MINIMIZE!" shouted Carter. "I want a FLASH transmission out to Tel-Aviv NOW, Mister, or you can kiss those bars on your shoulder goodbye! Send it to everybody we've got in the region. I want to know Israel's intentions."

"General Carter? Colonel Rawlins. I just landed at Dulles. I have some extremely interesting information from Nelson Medway. I'll be at your office in thirty minutes."

"Make it twenty, Colonel. I've got some news for you too."

With the offer of a fifty dollar tip on his mind, the taxi driver turned on his radar detector and flew down the Dulles access road toward Washington. Zack made good on his offer as the cab screeched to a halt twenty minutes later at the underground Pentagon entrance.

Adrenaline pumping, Zack hurried into the DCI's office. "General, I think I found..."

"Sit down, Zack," interrupted Carter. "The Israelis lost another settlement to a BW attack, and they retaliated with a tactical nuclear strike on military targets in the Bekaa."

Rawlins sat, momentarily stunned. "So what's the situation now?"

"Its a very tenuous Mexican standoff," replied Carter. "Our satellite shots from a few minutes ago show the Israelis have their fingers on the triggers of at least twenty more nukes, but they are holding back. Meanwhile, their country is ringed by perhaps a couple hundred SCUD-Bs, quite possibly armed with the same BW agent, and many capable of hitting Tel-Aviv."

"Well they have good reason to be concerned about such an attack," said Rawlins. "I believe the Russians have used Multiplex technology to develop a weaponized *E. coli* that can kill ethnic Jews with surgical precision, and it is being deployed by Fath and other forces in the region."

"Surgical precision, eh?" said Carter.

"Yes, Sir. The engineering of the bug is based on a genetic susceptibility unique to..."

"Then how do you explain ten Swedish members of the International Peacekeeping Force killed by this bug?" interrupted Carter. "About as surgically precise as a chain saw, I'd say."

"Why Colonel Rawlins," said the stewardess as Zack stepped aboard United 106, "didn't we just bring you home yesterday?"

"Yes, and its so nice to see you again. In fact, I enjoyed the flight so much I thought I'd have another go at it." Brushing past her puzzled expression, Zack moved efficiently to his window seat. It was 7:30 in the morning, nearly breakfast time, but he didn't feel hungry. In fact, his biological clock had been reset so many times in the last week he didn't know how he felt. In his seat, Zack went through the all-too-familiar motions. Fasten seatbelt securely, raise seatback to the full upright position, check to make sure meal tray is secured. As the stewardess began her mandatory safety speech, Zack's eyes closed. He felt some vague obligation to pay attention, though he could recite the entire presentation by heart. The flight attendant seemed equally disconnected from the demonstration. Gingerly easing the life preserver over her perfectly coiffed hair, she pulled the device down onto her shoulders. The manual inflation demonstration using the mouth tube, the only part of the show Rawlins ever really watched, was a bust. The risk to her lip gloss was just too great.

As the 747 rose over Dulles and began the slow turn to the northeast to head up the coast, Zack closed his eyes and thought about Sally.

"Why doesn't she ever get pissed—tell me she's not going to take it anymore, that she's going to leave?" When Zack had returned last night, only to be ordered by General Carter to be on the next morning's flight back to Tel-Aviv, he agonized over what to tell his wife. Over dinner at the kitchen table he avoided eye contact, a signal Sally readily picked up.

Vainly hoping to head off the inevitable, she said, "Zack, you've really been putting in a lot of hours lately, with all the TDY. Why don't we do something fun this weekend? The Navy's Blue Angels and the Golden Knights parachute team are performing at Andrews Air Force Base Saturday. Let's take the kids and go see them." It was unfair, of course, because she sensed what was coming. Perhaps it was a form of passive-aggression, her way of dealing with the situation.

"Great, just great," thought Rawlins as he realized the situation was only getting worse. "Sally, I'm afraid I'm going to have to leave again…tomorrow. Its really a very important matter, and very serious." His voice was a recording. Flat. Completely disengaged. Zack wanted to jump up and run out of the room. He just wanted to be…*not here.*

His wife stared at him in silence for two seconds before her eyes dropped with a sigh. "Its OK, Zack, I understand."

The chime announcing that smoking was now permitted jolted him back to the present. He immediately detected the faint smell of burning tobacco, as anxious smokers responded in Pavlovian fashion. How many miles was he logging on this commuter consulting? If he were only allowed to accumulate air-miles credits, he would have a couple of free trips to Europe by now for himself and Sally. Any other businessman or private citizen could accept the free flights, but not military personnel on orders. Rawlins figured there probably was a reason for the restriction, but it just didn't seem fair.

"Major," came Captain Steinberg's voice over the intercom, "can you come down to the lab for a minute? I've found something I think you should see."

"I'll be right down, David."

As he entered Lab Five's isolation suite, Samuels noted the Captain bent over one of the individual isolation boxes, concentrating on two Petri dishes containing bacterial cultures.

"These are two isolates from Mossat-Bar," said Steinberg, without looking up.

Samuels peered through the glass shield and studied the two dishes of agar, each covered with thousands of tiny bacterial colonies. His trained eyes readily detected subtle yet distinct differences in the appearance of the colonies on the two plates.

"That's *E. coli* on the left, and what's this other one, *Pseudomonas*?"

"Yes, Sir," replied Steinberg. "We found them both in the Mossat-Bar water supply. I checked this *E. coli* isolate with a DNA probe for the mutant toxin gene, and it is positive."

"Well that's bad news," said Samuels, "but pretty much what we expected to find, wouldn't you say?"

"Yes, Sir, but that's not the worst of it. The probe for the mutant gene identified the *Pseudomonas* as well."

"What? Are you sure? Did you run the proper controls?"

"Of course!" came the indignant reply.

"I'm sorry, David, I didn't mean to insult you. Its just that, I mean, our probes are so specific. How could a probe for an *E. coli* gene react with a *Pseudomonas* that lacks the gene?"

"Precisely..."

"Gene transfer?"

"There's no other explanation. I've repeated the hybridization analysis three times, and the probe for the mutant gene lights up the *Pseudomonas* every time. Of course this is not without precedent. Gene transfer between species occurs all the time in nature—it's how genetic diversity is maintained."

"Is the *Pseudomonas* actually producing the toxin?"

"I don't know that yet. We're running an anticholinesterase assay right now. I should have the results by 1400. I'm sure you understand the problem here, Major. All K-12 strain *E. coli*, including this mutant, are 'cripples,' engineered to be incapable of surviving for long outside of the laboratory, so an accidental release to the environment would be self-limiting within a day or so. Ultraviolet wavelengths in sunlight damage bacterial DNA. Since K-12's DNA-repairing enzymes have been deleted through genetic engineering, the damage is lethal to the bacteria. The *Pseudomonas*, however, do not have this limitation. They are well adapted to the environment, and can be found just about anywhere. They are also 'opportunists' that will infect a wide range of animal hosts, including man."

"Could this mutant gene transfer into other bacteria? I mean, how far can this process go?"

"That's hard to say, but judging by the speed and efficiency of this initial transfer, I'd say the gene must have been inserted into the *E. coli* on a transposon." Transposable elements, or transposons, were small pieces of DNA that spontaneously "jumped" between chromosomes, inserting and removing themselves at will, by an unknown mechanism. "You know, Sir," observed Steinberg, "this thing may be a little hard to control."

Samuels tried to focus on the danger, and how to deal with this terrible threat to all humanity. At the same time, he tried to block other thoughts about his own role in offensive biological weapons development. Despite being signatories to the 1972 BW Convention, Israel had maintained an active offensive program, based in Lab Five. He was sickened when he thought about his work on new killer microbes, but he was a soldier, and obedience to orders was preeminent. Young Captain Sternberg also never shared his thoughts on the subject with his superior, and worked efficiently and obediently to develop newer and more lethal microbes for the defense of Israel.

"Come in Zack," said the Defense Minister as Rawlins opened the door. Shoram could see, over the Colonel's shoulder, the ever-present scowl on Mrs. Raebel's face. "And close the door, please. I'm glad you were willing to return on such short notice. I've asked Major Samuels here to answer any technical questions you may have."

Willing, thought Rawlins, *not exactly the word I would have used.* "No problem, Sir. General Carter says things have heated up quite a bit in the last few days."

"Zack, the situation is grave. I'm not sure exactly how much you know, so I'll brief you. Terrorists hit another one of our settlements with BW, the same weaponized ***E. coli*** used at Tafiz. We had fifty civilian casualties, along with ten Swedish soldiers from the International Peacekeeping Force. In analyzing samples from the site of the most recent attack, Major Samuels has discovered a potentially even more serious complication. Major?"

"Yes, Sir. First, I should tell you that we just finished sequencing the toxin gene in this bug and it appears to have mutated even further. At this point we are just not sure what effects that might have on actual toxin production. However what concerns me much more than the weaponized *E. coli* is the fact that we found in the same water samples a *Pseudomonas* that also contains the mutant toxin gene. Captain Steinberg thinks the gene transferred spontaneously into the new host on a transposon."

"Transposon, eh?" replied Rawlins. "So you think the mutant gene was originally engineered into the *E. coli* by transposon mutagenesis? We could be dealing with a much higher-tech bug here than I thought."

"It looks that way. That would have been the easiest way to construct the mutant strain."

"And it also would produce the most unstable construction," interrupted Rawlins. Transposons, by their nature, moved around quite easily between chromosomes and between different organisms. Although a good molecular biologist could quickly mutate bacteria by this method, it was difficult to predict what subsequent changes might be induced in the mutant strain, particularly outside of a controlled laboratory environment.

"We are checking the *Pseudomonas* to see if it is actually producing the toxin," continued Samuels, "and we are sequencing the gene on the Multiplex, to see if it matches the *E. coli* gene exactly."

"Well I have several more pieces of the puzzle for you," said Rawlins, "but first I have been instructed by General Carter to ask you what your intentions are with respect to the hostile forces to the north and east."

"I'm sure your satellites reported the nuclear strikes we carried out," said Shoram. "You must understand it was a purely defensive response to the aggressive moves of our enemies."

"Yes, but nuclear missiles?"

"Zack, these people want to kill us. They want to kill me, they want to kill my family, they want to kill very Jew in Israel. I know our targets were not just military barracks, or missile sites, and I have little doubt that hundreds, perhaps thousands of civilians died, and I hate that." Raising a tightly clenched fist, the Minister continued, "But you must understand that the situation in Israel is very different from your country, where your neighbors are friendly and you have several thousand miles of ocean as a buffer zone on either border. Distances are much shorter here and we would have at best less than five minutes warning for an attack. On top of that our military communications system suffered a major casualty that has really crippled us."

"That brings up the other issue I need to ask you about," said Rawlins. "The disk you gave me with the sequence data you needed modeled was apparently infected with a virus. It severely damaged the Pentagon's main system and several of our users, and it wiped out Dan Reynolds' Cray at Cal-Tech. Now it sounds like it may have hit you too. How could Dov Messer let something like that happen?"

"You're right about a virus, Zack, and I am terribly sorry to hear that it got into your system. I do not know how we could have prevented it. It apparently was inside Lab Five's system, and really knocked us out. Dov is determined to find how it got past our vaccine programs, but right now he is concentrating on getting us back on line. Let me explain something to you, Zack. After Dov took over, I approved a proposal of his to consolidate our military communication network under Lab Five's computer system. His plan increased communication speed by a factor of ten, enhanced command and control from my office, and was projected to save us over five million dollars a year."

*Such a deal...*thought Rawlins.

"Although at first I was a little leery about putting all our eggs in one basket," continued Shoram, "Dov convinced me that the new system was failsafe. I took a gamble on the new technology, and lost, and I take full responsibility for it."

Rawlins felt vaguely uncomfortable about the situation. Shoram was the Defense Minister, and ultimately responsible for all defense matters, but Dov Messer seemed to be getting off awfully easy. In addition, the "whiz kid" had been working for over two days on repairing the damage, yet not a single subsystem was operational. Zack decided to bite the bullet.

"Minister Shoram, don't you think it's a little coincidental? I mean, the deployment of this new BW agent by Fath, the hostile military actions by Syria and Lebanon, and now a catastrophic failure of your new 'failsafe' military communications system?"

"What are you suggesting, Colonel?"

"And why is it taking your computer operations staff so long to get even a part of your system back? Those are the very best computer people you have in all of Israel."

The Defense Minister stared hard at Rawlins. His eyes flashed briefly to Major Samuels, then back to the Colonel.

Sensing the reaction, Rawlins hammered his message home. "These events appear to be strategically coordinated. I think you have an internal security problem."

There was an awkward pause, then Major Samuels responded, "The Colonel may be right, Sir, and now with Ana's death..."

"Ana?" asked Rawlins.

"Ana Weisner. She was the day shift supervisor in Lab Five. She was killed by a car bomb yesterday."

"Internal Affairs, Mr. Revich's office."

"This is Minister Shoram's office," said Mrs. Raebel brusquely. "The Minister would like Mr. Revich to come up to his office immediately." Arielle relished such phone calls. She loved announcing herself as "Minister Shoram's office." It conferred a greater-than-life stature that facilitated making outrageous impositions on other people's time.

"Mr. Revich is just leaving for another meeting," said the secretary. "May I have him..."

"The Minister insists," said Mrs. Raebel ominously, as she sharply replaced the receiver.

"Mr. Revich to see you, Sir."

"Send him in."

The door opened and the Director of Internal Affairs hurried in. He was a physically small man, and nervous by nature, so being summoned abruptly to the Defense Minister's office did nothing to calm him.

"You know about Ana Weisner, Lev," stated the DM.

"Yes, Sir, terrible."

"I want you to put someone on it immediately."

Revich looked surprised. Car bombings were tragic, and in Israel, tragically common. However the murder of a civilian employee outside of normal working hours, not on government property...it was hardly his department's responsibility. Considering his current backlog of investigations, Lev decided to risk a challenge. With beads of sweat now appearing on his forehead he asked, "Don't you think this is a matter for the police?"

"The bombing, perhaps," replied Shoram, "but I believe there may be more to this than random terrorism. Ana worked for Lab Five, which by the way, will limit who you can assign to the case. We have reason to suspect that our recent comm system failure was sabotage and that Ana, as a shift supervisor, may have stumbled upon the perpetrator."

Revich could see that he had another investigation on his hands and further, since he was the only employee in internal affairs cleared for Lab Five, that it was going to be his personal investigation.

"Dov Messer? Lev Revich, Internal Affairs. I've heard so much about you, its a pleasure to finally meet you. I also have never had the chance to thank you personally for your help in setting up our Local Area Network. The LAN is working perfectly. I don't know how we ever ran the department without it."

Dov eyed his visitor suspiciously. "We're here to help," he replied. This was clearly not a social call. Internal affairs were the guys with the black hats, and just the fact that Revich was here, inside Lab Five, meant trouble. "Was there something in particular you needed?"

"Actually, yes. I'd like to look at your shift records for the last two weeks."

"I'm sorry, but do you have some authorization for this?"

"Of course, Dov. May I call you Dov? Oh, and I'll need some assistance from one of your technicians, someone who thoroughly understands the system."

"Everyone here thoroughly understands the system," retorted Dov coldly.

"Here," said Revich as he handed Messer the memo signed by the Defense Minister.

Messer read the memo carefully. The DM had ordered an audit of computer operations records, ostensibly to uncover any slip in procedures that may have allowed a virus to penetrate the system from the outside. The auditor would find no slip. Dov had seen to that. Ana had come close, too close, but she was no longer a problem.

Chapter 11

"I have good news, Comrade Director. Dr. Salim has solved the stability problem with her construct. She believes the organism is now ready for mass production."

"Excellent!" replied Kostyakova. "Set up round-the-clock operations immediately. I want one thousand individual, sealed aliquots boxed up for shipment within three days."

Anatoly Steklov, Chief Scientist at the Kirishi Agricultural Institute, was momentarily stunned. He had expected an enthusiastic reaction to the news by the head of Minmedbioprom, but not a demand for a thousand vials of the dangerous pathogenic organism, safely packaged and ready to deliver in days.

"Is there a problem?" asked Kostyakova as he read the anxiety in Steklov's face.

"Certainly, Comrade Director, we have the capability. It is just that..."

"Just what?" demanded Kostyakova.

"Well, personnel. As you know, we only have a small staff authorized to work on this project. We cannot support a scaled-up, twenty-four operation with so few technicians."

"Well then clear some more people!" ordered the Director. "Pull them from another department. How about those slugs in the wheat program? Take a dozen of them and do backgrounds on them. Tell security I want all the clearances within twenty four hours."

"Of course, comrade, I can get clearance. However I am more concerned about training. That is something that cannot be rushed, and we are not fermenting yogurt here."

"Enough of your insolence!" thundered Kostyakova. "You are to obey orders, not question them! I understand the risks involved. It is you who do not understand the importance of this project. I take full responsibility for this decision. Have the list of new technicians on my desk by tomorrow afternoon."

Chief Scientist Steklov scurried out like a whipped dog. He clearly had misjudged the Director's priorities. Kostyakova had once been a leading scientist, but now he was a consummate politician. *Follow policy, carry out orders, no matter the cost.* He would carry out the orders, he had no choice, but he was terrified of the possible consequences. The genetically engineered bacterium Dr. Salim's team had produced was by far the most dangerous microorganism he had ever seen. More unsettling however, was the demonstrated instability of the organism. Nayah Salim had designed a mutated version of the *E. coli* toxin gene, whose product specifically targeted an enzyme variant found in many ethnic Jews. She had then engineered the mutated gene into the K-12 strain of *E. coli*, replacing the natural, innocuous form of the gene in the bacteria. The problem was that as the bacteria reproduced, the transposon on which the mutant gene was located tended to move around within the chromosome. It was this unpredictable, spontaneous relocation of the tox gene that concerned Steklov. Depending on where the gene turned up, there could be secondary effects that were completely unknown.

Nayah had tried to assure Anatoly that she had been able to fix the position of the tox gene, and that the stability problem was solved. What her data actually demonstrated however, was merely that after several bacterial generations, the gene appeared to remain in the same position. So despite his concerns over biosafety and the need for additional testing, Steklov implemented the twenty-four hour production schedule demanded by Kostyakova. Workers were pulled from other projects, given a two hour indoctrination lecture, and ordered to read the procedure manual used in Salim's laboratory. Within forty-eight hours the first samples, one-milliliter aliquots of bacteria freeze dried in small glass ampoules, began coming off the laboratory production line.

The courier from the Lebanese embassy delivered the confidential message to Fath headquarters, where it was rushed to Ibn Nimr. Inside the sealed diplomatic envelope was a short message from Dr. Salim, countersigned by Kostyakova. The full lot of the product was being prepared, and would be delivered on schedule, according to the plan.

"It is done," murmured Ibn Nimr as he slid the message into the shredder beside his desk. The "free samples" he had been given of this new weapon worked perfectly as predicted. Now, a thousand times as much was his to use against Israel. The thought of that kind of power energized him. With Israel's military communication system now destroyed, and the super weapon soon in his hands, Operation Majdi would proceed. His smile widened as, ironically, the Zionist tale of David and Goliath came to his mind.

"Thank you for agreeing to meet with me, General Vankovich," said Colonel Rawlins.

"This meeting is most irregular," responded the General. "As you no doubt know, Service B in the First Directorate of the KGB is responsible for internal security within Russia. So I fail to see what a foreign intelligence officer like yourself and I have to talk about."

"I think that will soon become clear," responded Rawlins. "Do you recall a statement by an official of your government two years ago that if the U.S. presses ahead on the Strategic Defense Initiative, Russia will counter asymmetrically with a threat based on genetic engineering? The official said your country will not copy any more, or play catch-up. If the U.S. develops something in space, Russia will develop something on the ground."

"Ah, yes, that statement created quite a stir," grinned the General. "However the statement did not reflect Russian policy, and the official who made it was promptly reassigned. In any event, that was over two years ago. Glasnost has changed everything. I can assure you that despite America's aggressive and provocative development of SDI, our country would never sanction development of new biological weapons. That is, I presume, what you are implying has happened, and the purpose of your visit."

"You are very astute, General Vankovich, but if that is in fact your official national policy then I submit to you that unsanctioned development of biological weapons is taking place in your country."

"And where might this unsanctioned BW development be taking place?"

"At the Kirishi Agricultural Research Institute."

"What evidence do you have in support of this claim?"

"A source in Kirishi leaked to Samizdat that the large bioreactor is being used to mass produce some kind of recombinant bacteria under biocontainment level *four* conditions."

"But that does not prove..."

"General," interrupted Rawlins, "listen to me. We have information that advance samples of this BW agent were supplied to a terrorist group in the Middle East, and that the material was used against Israel. Why do you think the Israelis nuked Lebanon last week—because some kids threw rocks at their soldiers? What's more, the source at Kirishi claims that two five-hundred unit shipments of the weapon are being produced and are being prepared for delivery tomorrow. Under the compliance terms of the Geneva treaty you must allow me to go to Kirishi to inspect the Institute. The shipment must be stopped."

"Come now, Colonel, why should we allow you to inspect our Institute? If it is as you say, we will find the shipment ourselves."

"General, the Kirishi Institute Bioreactor facility produces large quantities of a variety of microorganisms, for a range of beneficial and entirely peaceful applications. We believe that this particular BW agent appears virtually identical to normal laboratory bacteria, and can only be identified by a highly specific sensor."

"And I suppose you possess such a sensor?"

Rawlins replied simply with a couple of pats on his briefcase.

"Major Samuels I have the assay results on the *Pseudomonas* isolate from Mossat-Bar and I'm afraid its not good. The tox gene is functional and the bug is every bit as active against acetylcholinesterase as the K-12 isolate. What's worse, the toxin this bug is pumping out appears to knock out all variants of the enzyme, regardless of the source."

"Let me understand," said Samuels. "You're saying that when the transposon jumped into this new bacterium, the toxin lost its original host specificity. Now it will destroy the enzyme in anyone, with equal effectiveness."

Captain Steinberg confirmed the Major's analysis with a steady stare.

"I hope you washed your hands, David."

"I am Colonel Petrenko!" bellowed Rawlins' escort. "I have orders from General Vankovich to conduct an inspection."

"I am sorry Comrade Colonel," stammered the young Corporal as he nervously fingered his Kalashnikov. "Director Kostyakova has ordered that no one except authorized Institute employees be allowed in without his expressed permission."

"Damn that bureaucratznik! Corporal, you call your Director and inform him of my breach of regulations, because we are going in now and I warn you, do not try to stop us."

Ignoring the snarling dogs behind the chainlink fences on either side, the two hurried in and headed for the windowless concrete structure that was the Molecular Biology Institute. Inside the guard, aroused from sleep, jumped to his feet in confusion.

The officer ended the conversation before it started. "I am Colonel Petrenko. I have orders from General Vankovich to inspect this facility.

Please bring your passkey and come with me. Take us first to Dr. Steklov's office. Is he in?"

"Yes, Sir, I mean, I saw him this afternoon."

The men's footsteps reverberated loudly down the marble floor of the long, empty corridor. Receiving no reply to his knock on the Chief Scientist's door, the guard cautiously cracked the door and peered in.

"He must be in the lab."

Too quiet, thought Rawlins as the elevator door opened at the entrance to the high containment suite in the basement. The two officers quickly approached the chrome steel door and peered through the narrow window slit. Fear swept over Rawlins as he spotted a human form in a white laboratory coat, slumped over a desk. From the door he could also see someone else's foot protruding out from beyond a lab bench.

The two turned to each other in disbelief. "Where are your BC-4 suits?" Petrenko asked the guard.

"In that room," he replied, pointing to a door on their right. "You must then enter the lab from that room, through the airlock."

"Shall we, Colonel Rawlins?" invited the Russian. "Do you have your sensor ready?"

Rawlins felt a slight pull of air as they opened the inner airlock to the negative-pressure lab. Stepping gingerly through the hatch in his BC-4 suit, Rawlins saw immediately the body of a young woman. Ten feet to her left lay another body and beyond that another. In less that a minute they located the entire five-man lab crew, all dead, but no Steklov. The technicians' faces were contorted, and several lay with their hands at their throats as if gasping for breath.

On a laboratory bench in one corner sat a shipping case that contained five hundred sealed ampoules. Rawlins couldn't read the Cyrillic characters on the label, but the international biohazard warning sign on the box told him all he needed to know. The second case that had reportedly been prepared was no where to be found.

Across the laboratory, Rawlins' gaze stopped abruptly, as his worst fears were confirmed. A completely assembled Multiplex system sat on a table. It looked so harmless, like just another piece of laboratory equipment. The instrument only did as it was programmed, but this instrument was programmed to do evil.

"Will you check these samples, Colonel Rawlins?" asked Petrenko.

"What? Sure, right now," replied Rawlins, as the Russian's voice redirected his thoughts to the case of vials. He placed his instrument case onto the benchtop, opened it and prepared the DNA sensor for operation. After standardizing the baseline on the display, he turned to the shipping case and gingerly removed the lid. Both men stopped, as they looked at the top tier of ampoules. So clean and orderly, the small identical glass vials appeared as harmless as a rack of test tubes. Rawlins could hardly bring himself to touch them. Such incredible power, such incredible danger. They seemed to express an almost palpable force that repelled his touch. He could sense Petrenko's encouragement, but his hand shook as he reached in and extracted a single vial. Snapping off the top of the vial at the scored constriction, Rawlins added exactly one milliliter of saline solution with a pipette. The fluffy white contents of the vial immediately dissolved into solution, and he transferred the vial onto the sensor. Slowly inserting the test probe into the vial, he pushed the run button. The machine quickly ran through its program and within seconds the LED display confirmed the identity of the sample. The vial contained K-12 *E. coli*, positive for the mutant toxin gene.

Rawlins stared at Colonel Petrenko through his facemask, and jerked his head toward the decon room exit.

"Let's skip the discussion, Colonel," said Rawlins as he struggled out of the cumbersome suit still dripping wet from the disinfectant shower. "There is nothing we can do here. We need to find Steklov and we need to find that other shipping case."

"Corporal, have you seen Dr. Steklov?" demanded Petrenko.

"Yes, Sir. I have been trying to contact you. Dr. Steklov left a few minutes ago, while you were inside. He ordered me to evacuate the Institute."

"What! And you just let him go?"

"Let him go? I did not know…."

"Never mind, you fool. Allow no one to enter the Institute until you hear from me personally, do you understand? Come Colonel Rawlins, we have much work to do."

The young guard, confused by strong forces he could not understand or control, stared dejectedly at the ground.

"Comrade Director we have a serious problem at Kirishi," stated Steklov. "One of General Vankovich's agents conducted a surprise inspection of the Molecular Biology Institute, accompanied by an American intelligence officer, and…"

"What!" roared Kostyakova. "An American…who authorized…do you realize what this could mean?"

"Comrade Director, if you will please allow me to continue." The presence of the American at Kirishi is awkward, but…:

"Awkward! Awkward? Steklov you idiot! This is a totally irresponsible breach of security. Get your Chief of Security. I want the name of every guard on duty at the time."

"Comrade Director," shouted the Chief Scientist, "listen to me. The foreigner is the least of our problems. There has been a bio-accident at the laboratory. The entire lab crew is dead."

"And the American?"

"He and his escort, a Colonel Petrenko, left the laboratory apparently unharmed after quizzing the guard about any shipments that had recently left the Institute. My staff checked the lab and found one case of Dr. Salim's product. A second case had apparently left the lab. I am very concerned about an accidental release of the organism, or perhaps a contaminated shipping container."

"The First Directorate must not have this information," hissed Kostyakova, "or we will both live out our lives in Siberia."

"But the shipment," cried Steklov. "If it is contaminated..."

"Enough of your whining! Those fools knew what they were buying. Let Allah protect them now." Quickly dialing a number on his telephone, the Director shouted into the receiver, "Kazarian, I want you in my office in five minutes."

Minutes later a knock sounded at the door.

"Come in," ordered Kostyakova.

The door swung open and a fat, evil-looking man wearing the uniform of a KGB Major stepped in.

"Good afternoon, Comrade Director," said Kazarian with a smirk. "How can I help you?"

By jumping into the Volga you Armenian swine, thought Kostyakova. He despised the KGB officer, but summoned him because he knew he could get the job done.

"An American intelligence officer, with the aid of a traitorous agent of General Vankovich has obtained information vital to national security. I believe they are still in St. Petersburg but I fear they may soon attempt to flee the country. This must not be allowed, nor may they be allowed to report back to their cronies in the First Directorate. Do I make myself clear?"

"Completely, Comrade Director. I will locate them and gain their full cooperation." The eyes in Kazarian's fat face leered at Steklov, seeking a reaction. It was obvious he relished such an assignment.

Steklov was appalled at what plainly was an order by the civilian head of Minmedbioprom for the summary execution of a foreign military officer and a KGB Colonel. As a scientist, he was even more appalled at the Director's callous disregard for innocent Russians who might die from accidental exposure to the bioweapon.

With a last leer at Steklov, Kazarian turned and hurried out the door, obviously energized by such a choice assignment.

"You see?" soothed Kostyakova. "You mustn't get so excited. The problem will soon be eliminated."

The shipping address on the case in the lab was 3 Pretlov Street, in St. Petersburg's warehouse district. The loading dock worker there told Colonel Petrenko that yes, a single case had arrived late last night from Kirishi, but he did not know what it contained. The shipment had been picked up immediately by a middle-eastern appearing man driving a black minivan. The consignee on the invoice was listed as "V. Stepanovich," but Rawlins was somehow not surprised to find that the address was an office of the Lebanese consulate.

Kazarian's three agents watched intently from their car as the two targets drove away from the warehouse. They had been told that the pair would be trying to flee St. Petersburg, so they were surprised to observe Petrenko's car pull over and stop. Before the agents could intervene the two men had left their car and entered a building.

"Comrade Major," called the leader over his radio, "the subjects have stopped and entered the Lebanese consulate."

"When they come out, kill them," came the emotionless response.

Lord Medway had been busy, placing a call directly to the Lebanese consulate in St. Petersburg. As a result, the duty officer was remarkably cooperative when Petrenko and Rawlins showed up unannounced. Nonetheless, the officer insisted that no shipment had been received from Kirishi. Stepping out of the office into the courtyard, both men stopped as they noticed the black minivan parked in a carport by the front wall. Petrenko hurried over to the van and peered in through the rear window.

"Empty."

"God help us," said Rawlins. "It's on its way."

Chapter 12

Dov Messer had accomplished his mission flawlessly. The one year assignment was to infiltrate Lab Five, consolidate military communications into what was effectively a "super-bottleneck" and kill the system. He was then to remain on site for forty-eight hours, ostensibly working on repairing the system, and evacuate to Fath headquarters in Beirut. Now at his flat, paranoia washed over him as he frantically grabbed a few last possessions. His entire life, since college, had been an incredible charade. When the real Dov Messer, a fellow student at Haifa University had died in a car accident while on summer break in Geneva, he had assumed Messer's identity. False identification papers were easy to obtain, and his student activism in support of Jewish settlements in the occupied territories was the perfect cover. Now it was finally over. The last twelve months had been almost too much for him. The Chanukah party, the despised yarmulke and the endless excuses why he never seemed to be seen at temple. Like the Phoenix, he was preparing to rise out of what was soon to be the rubble of Israel. He would resume his former life and his former name, Ahmed Al-Habar.

Petrenko had been on too many stakeouts himself to miss noticing the KGB agents parked across the street. He pretended not to notice the three men approaching briskly as he and Rawlins got into their car.

"What…?" exclaimed Rawlins as Petrenko reached under the seat and extracted two semi-automatic pistols.

"We have company."

The Russian Colonel was himself KGB and he knew their methods—knew there would be only one chance.

"Comrade Colonel," said the leader, "you will..."

The order was cut short as a burst of bullets from Petrenko's pistol tore off half his head. Turning slightly and firing again, the Colonel dropped the second agent as he reached for his weapon. On the other side of the car, the third agent fired and Rawlins heard Petrenko grunt. Rawlins reacted instinctively, ducking and grabbing the second pistol off the seat. He reached over his head and blindly unloaded the clip out the window.

With no return fire from outside the car, Rawlins cautiously peered over the window edge. The third agent lay sprawled in a pool of blood, struck by at least five bullets.

"Not bad," he observed. "Just think what I could have done if I had my eyes open."

Petrenko's groan pulled Rawlin's attention back inside the car.

"Let's see where you're hit," said Rawlins.

"Just my shoulder," answered Petrenko. "Its a good thing they do not train KGB officers the way they did in my day. If I had planned this hit, we would both be dead."

"They were KGB?" asked Rawlins. "Why were they after us, and who would have given the orders?"

"They are Kazarian's men. Common thugs who shame the KGB, like the bloated fool they follow. You can count on them to shoot first and ask questions later. This is big, Colonel Rawlins, and Kostyakova is at the top. We cannot hope to stop this operation unless we can tie him in, and I think I know how to do it."

"Why don't we just go to General Vankovich directly?" protested Rawlins as they sped away from the carnage.

"Colonel, you do not understand. In my country you do not even trust your mother. By now Kostyakova will have convinced everyone including the General that you and I are spies, attempting to escape with information that will cripple our country. Those agents back there were not sent to interview us. We are dead men."

"Establish roadblocks on every highway out of St. Petersburg," Vankovich instructed calmly, "and place agents at the airport and train station." Replacing the telephone, the General turned back to his visitor. "They cannot escape, Comrade Director. Now, tell me exactly what you are doing at Kirishi, and why these two would want to mislead me."

"As you know, Comrade General, the 1973 treaty in Geneva banned production, stockpiling and use of all biological weapons worldwide. Our great nation of course complied fully with all terms of this treaty, while the United States continued and even accelerated development of such weapons." Noting the frown on Vankovich's face, Kostyakova continued, "This information is compartmentalized, and in Service B you would not have access to it, but I can assure you it is accurate. Some time ago the Americans began working on the development of a 'super-pathogen,' a biological weapon for which no countermeasure exists, and a few months ago they succeeded. When we learned of this I was tasked with using the Kirishi facility to develop a vaccine to counter this threat. Our scientists have recently produced an effective vaccine and this formulation is what your Colonel Petrenko and the American spy now seek to deliver to the West. Since American vaccine production capability vastly exceeds that of our own, we believe they will mass produce our vaccine, immunize their troops, and then use their insidious weapon with impunity against our country."

"This is incredible," replied Vankovich. "However if there is even a chance that it is true, they must be stopped."

"I assure you, Comrade General, this information is one hundred per cent reliable. Trust me."

"The KGB will have roadblocks on all major highways by now and they will be covering the airport and train station. It is time for me to call in a favor."

Rawlins was puzzled by the Colonel's remark, but if the Russian had an angle, Rawlins was all for it.

"You better let me drive," said Rawlins as he noticed the car's unsteady progress down the road.

"No, we are almost there."

Petrenko turned the car abruptly into a narrow alley, maneuvering past large boxes of trash, and stopped.

"Where are we?" asked Rawlins.

"You have heard of Samizdat, I trust?"

The intelligence officer hesitated instinctively, but the fugitive realized that this was no time for games.

"Yes, of course."

"This is the house of Vitaly Skurnik. He is a baker by day but his nights are spent organizing and distributing dissident literature for Samizdat." Petrenko looked at Rawlins for a reaction. "Perhaps you are wondering why we have not arrested him."

"You doubtless have your reasons."

"Indeed. Comrade Skurnik actually provides a service to me. The information he distributes, while embarrassing to many of our local and national leaders, is hardly a threat to national security. I like to think of him as a sort of pressure release valve for the people. We both know of each other's operations and we leave each other alone. It maintains a sort of balance. His daughter and mine, in fact, are schoolmates. But enough talk. We must get inside."

"Wait, let me help you," insisted Rawlins as he saw the Colonel wince in pain as he tried to exit the car.

Responding to their knock, the wooden door opened a fraction of an inch.

"Yes?" came the cautious reply.

Petrenko could not see the speaker in the darkness beyond the narrow crack.

"Tell Vitaly that Petrenko is here to see him."

The door shut with no reply, then re-opened a minute later.

"Come in," said the woman, eyeing them suspiciously. "Vitaly will be down shortly." Noticing the Colonel's blood-soaked jacket, her expression softened. "You are hurt. Please, sit down. I will get some bandages."

"Comrade Petrenko," called the old man from the top of the stairs, "it has been a long time—too long. Am I under arrest?" Both men laughed loudly, causing the Colonel to recoil in pain.

"What has happened to you? You are hurt. And who is your friend?"

"We were attacked by Kazarian's men."

"Do you think they followed you here?"

"Do not fear, they will not be following anyone, anywhere. This is Colonel Rawlins. He is an American."

Skurnik stroked his thick gray beard and sized up the situation. "You have killed some of Kazarian's men and got yourself shot in the process. Now you come to my house in broad daylight, accompanied by an American military officer. I would say you have big problems, Comrade Petrenko."

"You are most astute, Comrade Skurnik."

Checking both directions on his street, Ahmed darted from his flat to his car. Speeding out of town to the east, he was anxious to put as many kilometers as possible between himself and the defense ministry. That little bloodhound, Revitch, had really been closing in on him. More importantly however, he knew that the stage was set for something big to happen in Israel, something devastating, and he would just as soon not be in Tel-Aviv when it did.

Distracted by the stress of his situation, Ahmed failed to notice the large truck full of kosher sausages pulling out into the street from a blind alley. The last thing he saw was the large Star of David on the side of the truck, as it slammed into his face at sixty miles per hour.

"The traitors have killed three of my officers," said Kazarian to the General. "However they are trapped in St. Petersburg and cannot escape.

With your permission, we will arrest Petrenko's family. They will lead us to the criminals." Beads of sweat dotted the fat man's high forehead as his lips stretched into a malevolent grin.

Vankovich already regretted putting Kazarian on the case. Torturing women and children was one of the Major's passions, exceeded only by his gluttony.

"No, Major, that will not be necessary. We will find them soon enough. That will be all."

Kazarian's mouth dropped open in protest, stretching the small flecks of foamy white saliva that had formed at the corners of his mouth, his disappointment obvious. Recovering quickly, his chubby body spun around adroitly and he marched obediently out of the room.

"There," soothed Skurnik's wife, "you will be fine."

"Thank you very much," replied the Colonel. "Now, old friend," as he turned to Skurnik, "here is the reason for my visit. As you and Samizdat have told the people, there is some question as to the nature of the research at Kirishi. Recently Israel was attacked by terrorists using biological weapons. Colonel Rawlins here believes that the weapons were in fact manufactured at the Molecular Biology Institute, and his government has sent him here to investigate."

Skurnick listened in disbelief. Here were an American intelligence officer and a KGB colonel, talking freely about exceptionally sensitive information, while sitting in Samizdat's "Information Central."

"This is...astounding. Who is behind this? Kostyakova? Why do you not go to General Vankovich?"

"Kostyakova got to him first," answered Rawlins. "He must have convinced the General that we were spies, because he's put Kazarian after us." Petrenko's good hand rose slowly to his wounded arm, in subconscious confirmation.

"But we are not the issue," continued Petrenko. "We are only a smoke screen for Kostyakova. The reality is that a terrible weapon has been produced at Kirishi, one that will de-stabilize the entire Middle East, and a shipment has already been sent."

"What can I do?" offered Skurnik.

"Colonel Rawlins and I must stop that shipment from reaching its destination and being deployed, and we need your help and the Samizdat network to get out of the country."

"Antisense DNA," said Steinberg. "That's how we will decon Mossat-Bar and stop the spread of this toxin gene." He and Major Samuels had been racking their brains for two days over how to recover the site. Blanketing the area with disinfectants or other toxic chemicals was unrealistic. Massive environmental treatment with antibiotics was also not an effective solution, because the unpredictable element of gene transfer made it impossible to know what organisms might now be carrying the toxin gene. The wrong choice of antibiotics would not only leave many bacteria unscathed, but might also select for an antibiotic resistant "super strain" that would only compound their problems.

"How would you propose to use antisense DNA?" asked Samuels.

"As you know," explained the Captain, "antisense DNA is short pieces of synthetic DNA designed to match and bind to specific genes or their messages, the 'sense' molecules, to shut down the function of the gene. Since we do not want or need to exterminate every living creature in Mossat-Bar we need an extremely specific method. With the Multiplex we can quickly design antisense DNA to target any organism that contains the toxin gene, and no other. Then it's just a matter of mixing the DNA with one of the stabilized emulsions we use in agricultural spraying and delivering it on target by chopper."

Major Samuels stared at Steinberg in open admiration. There was no question his ERT had "the right stuff." The solution was so high tech, so elegant, yet the Captain made it sound so easy. With the proper antisense reagent, they could reach into a mixed pool of a million bacteria and strike out a single bug containing the target gene.

"So what do you say, Major. Think it's a good idea?"

"A good idea?" repeated Samuels, as he drifted back into the moment. "Yes, David, its a great idea." *Damn, I love this job.*

"I have sent for a friend," said Skurnik. "He will help you."

Soon there was a knock at the door and the woman hurried to answer it.

"Come in, Sergei."

"Sergei Gordaleyev," said Skurnik, "this is Colonel Rawlins from the United States, and you know Colonel Petrenko. They have come here with some information that corroborates what you told me some time ago. Kirishi is indeed being used for BW production and a large shipment of a new weapon has just been sent to terrorists in the Middle East."

"Surely General Vankovich would not tolerate such insanity," exclaimed Sergei. "Colonel Petrenko, have you not reported this?"

"It is too late for that," replied Skurnik. "Kostyakova has twisted the truth, three of Kazarian's enforcers have been killed and there is no going back. These men must get out of the country immediately."

"So Boris was right," said Sergei. "I knew it."

"Boris?" inquired Petrenko.

"Boris Dutrev. He is a close friend of mine who worked at Kirishi. He told me some time ago that he feared the Molecular Biology Institute was producing BW agents. I brought this information to Samizdat and two days later Boris was arrested. No one has heard from him since."

"This is incredible," said Petrenko. "In my own district! Arrests and disappearances just do not occur without my knowledge. Kostyakova is responsible for this. He has become far too powerful, he must be stopped. Comrade Gordaleyev, get us out of the country, help us stop this weapon, and I will find your friend."

Chapter 13

"Tonight." reported Ben Nabul over the telephone. "The first shipment will arrive by boat, twenty miles north of Haifa. Then by car to the transfer point in the city. The remaining shipment will be delivered tomorrow night."

"Excellent," replied Ibn Nimr. The head of Fath eased back in his chair with a satisfied smile. His expression was soft, almost kind, and stood as counterpoint to the incredible evil he had created in Operation Majdi. Nimr was clever, some said brilliant, but all his thoughts and all his energy were focused on one thing—the destruction of Israel. A devout Muslim, he never failed to make time for prayers, and now he prayed for strength, for Fath and for Majdi. Somehow it did not seem inconsistent to him to solicit the aid of a benevolent and merciful God in carrying out the genocide of a people.

"Here are your new passports, gentlemen," said Sergei proudly, and then he smiled. "Careful, do not smear the ink."

"Percy Whitesides," Rawlins read aloud. "Percy?" Somehow Zack couldn't picture himself as a "Percy," even though the name seemed to fit the British passport. His new employer was British Petroleum and his new business associate, Alexander Voshin, was a representative of the Russian Energy Council. After a quick change of clothing they thanked their hosts and prepared to leave.

Sergei opened the door and led the two businessmen out toward the waiting car. The first three bullets caught Sergei square in the chest, slamming him backwards against the rough stone of the house. Rawlins and Petrenko dove for cover behind the car, as bullets ricocheted off the cobblestone street around them. They were trapped in a crossfire and, being military men, they both knew that as soon as their assailants realized that they were unarmed, it would be all over. With some shouted words from a doorway across the street, the hail of gunfire abruptly ceased, and two of Kazarian's agents stepped out in the open. Quickly approaching the prone figures, they ordered them to get up.

Get up, lie down–what does it matter? Thought Zack. Slowly rising on one knee, his legs tensed in preparation for a desperate lunge at the men with guns, Zack flinched instinctively as he heard the expected sound of gunfire. The two goons looked shocked, then staggered, and dropped their guns, as they pitched forward to the street. Seeing the pool of blood spreading around the fallen men, Rawlins finally realized that what he had heard was "friendly fire."

"Hurry, you must go," shouted Vitaly from the balcony over Zack's head. "I'll take you."

Zack looked up to see Skurnik pull his Kalashnikov back from the flower planter full of geraniums, and disappear into the upstairs bedroom.

Pulling on his coat as he exited the house, Skurnik asked, "Are you both alright?"

"No new wounds," replied Petrenko sarcastically, as he held his bandaged shoulder.

Vitaly turned to them, "When we get to the airport there will be guards looking for you but do not fear, they will not have any photographs and your papers are in order. You are both booked on Aeroflot 1002 to Berlin. From there I am afraid you are on your own."

"Vitaly," said Petrenko seriously, "you have served your country and the Russian people more than you will ever know, and I am grateful. When I return, and I will return, we will find Sergei's friend, Boris. I will also bring evidence that will stop Kostyakova and his plans. I only hope we can stop his weapon."

At the St. Petersburg airport Rawlins, who was to check in first, got out at the south terminal. Petrenko, who would walk back and check in fifteen minutes later, continued on to the north terminal.

"Good luck, Colonel," said Sergei as Petrenko left the car. "We would have made a good team."

As Rawlins made his way through the disorderly crowd in the lobby he felt as if he were carrying a sign that proclaimed *American spy.* He didn't look Russian, he didn't feel British and he wasn't at all sure he could answer without hesitation to the name Percy. So, effecting what he hoped was a most arrogant British expression, he raised his chin and walked confidently past the suspicious stares of the gray-uniformed guards.

"Berlin, Mr. Whitesides?" asked the plain-looking Aeroflot agent.

"Yes. No smoking, please," replied Zack, in an accent that would have made Nelson Medway cringe. His "U.K. accent," as he called it, was a unique blend of British, Australian and Scottish sounds and expressions spoken like no one else on Earth. At least it was English, sort of, and Rawlins was sure the average Russian would buy it.

Looking down the lobby Rawlins' heart sank as he saw Petrenko, stopped, his path blocked by two guards. The Colonel was talking to the guards and showing them his papers. After an agonizing few minutes the guards returned Petrenko's papers and allowed him to proceed, watching him closely as he walked toward the Aeroflot counter.

Rawlins snatched his boarding pass, a little too quickly, and moved away from the counter as Petrenko approached. Their eyes met briefly but revealed no sign of recognition as they passed. *One hour to boarding time...*

Faka strained his eyes over the moonless Mediterranean Sea, looking for a response to his signal. The boat was late, more than half an hour. Another twenty minutes and an Israeli patrol jeep would be making its rounds past the rocky cove where he waited to receive the shipment. He had served as pickup man for countless smuggled shipments including drugs, people, jewelry, even non-kosher foods, but this one he did not like at all. It was all too secret, and the rumors about Russians...Once more his red light flashed out to sea. There! A faint red flash, then two, then one again. The signal.

It seemed like another hour before the small boat skidded up onto the beach. The boat operator exchanged a few words with Faka and quickly passed the case to him, before shoving his boat back into the sea to be absorbed by the night. The shipment now his responsibility, Faka hurried up the path to the car, his thoughts focused on the return drive to Haifa. Just as he reached the vehicle, daylight erupted in a brilliant spotlight, and an amplified voice ordered him to halt.

The Israeli patrol! Faka could only react. He dropped the case, fell to the ground and unleashed a burst from his Uzi in the direction of the voice. The spotlight exploded and faded into a smoking red glow. Return fire kicked up sand all around him, but he continued firing until the clip was empty. As the echo of his last round rebounded past him off the nearby cliffs, he realized he was no longer taking fire from the patrol. His aim had been lucky, and deadly.

The shipment box had been hit by several Israeli rounds but appeared to be intact. Faka quickly grabbed the case and tossed it into the trunk of his car. "Son of a pig!" he cursed, as glass shards on the outside of the damaged case sliced his right thumb. He jumped into the driver's seat and awkwardly started the car with his left hand. Flooring the accelerator up the bumpy road and onto the highway south, he unconsciously sucked on his bleeding thumb as his thoughts returned to his assignment.

"Aeroflot flight number 1002 to Berlin is now ready for boarding at gate thirteen," came the announcement in barely understandable English. Rawlins resisted the temptation to look at Petrenko, who sat quietly reading a newspaper a few feet away. He stood slowly, taking a moment to straighten his clothes. *Mustn't be in a hurry, mustn't look too anxious.* Trying to look tired and bored, Zack grasped his bag and moved past Petrenko, merging with the crowd shuffling into the bottleneck at the gate.

Once aboard, he sidestepped down the narrow aisle, negotiating a path through an endless array of obstacles. Short, stocky women wearing babushkas blocked the aisle while they attempted in vain to force oversized, shabby packages into the tiny overhead compartments. Other bags and packages of all sizes and shapes, apparently abandoned by their owners, projected treacherously out into the walkway. Still other people simply stood in the aisle, as if awaiting governmental instructions to be seated.

"At least I was able to get a no smoking..." Rawlins paused, as he confirmed the number of his empty middle seat between two Russians, both barely visible behind thick clouds of cigarette smoke. He glanced pointedly at the nearest flight attendant, a frustrated appeal that was met only with the impassive stare of a jaded employee in a subsidized business.

Zack was relieved to see Petrenko settling in a few rows forward, but it wasn't until the landing gear shuddered closed and the flaps whirred back into the wings that he closed his eyes and let his taught shoulders drop a little. *The shipment...*Rawlins' mind raced, as the gravity of the problem erased his personal discomfort.

Faka drove carefully, he dared not risk being stopped. Besides, his right hand ached with the cut he had sustained from the broken glass vials in the damaged crate. Approaching Haifa, Faka felt that something was wrong. The blur of distant city lights was becoming no clearer as he approached. In fact, he was having trouble focusing his eyes. Finding the correct address in the dark, narrow streets was hard enough, but especially so as he was beginning to feel quite ill. Turning down an unpaved alley, he was relieved to see the painted number of his destination on the wall beside a rusty iron gate. Faka sounded the horn once, then three times quickly, then once more, and he waited. By now he was having trouble breathing. The gate creaked slowly inward and he pulled the car into the driveway.

"Allahuakhbar. The shipment is in the trunk," he said to the guard. "Please, my brother, will you return with some water? And be careful of the box, it has some broken glass."

The guard nodded as he stepped back and removed the case from the trunk. When he returned with the water, he found the driver slumped over the steering wheel, a confused expression draining from his lifeless eyes.

Chapter 14

Back at Lab Five, Captain Steinberg had just completed a forty-eight hour synthesis run to make enough antisense DNA to neutralize the toxin gene contaminating Mossat-Bar, when Major Samuels showed up.

"How is it going, David?"

"Fine, Sir. We have all the antisense, and I'll have it in the sprayer on the chopper within an hour. Then we're off to the site."

"Can we get nanomolar concentrations in the water supply?" asked the Major.

"Yes, Sir, easily," replied Steinberg, "and we'll saturate a one hundred meter radius around the reservoir as well. For good measure, I plan on dusting the entire village with the remaining DNA."

"This better do it," warned Samuels. "With a gene that unstable, it may be unstoppable if it gets anywhere near a major population center."

At the drop point in Haifa, the men expediting the shipment gathered nervously to stare at the box sitting on the table under the harsh incandescent bulb. Through a damaged corner of the crate, small glass vials could be seen, aligned in neat rows. A few were broken, but most were intact, and each appeared to contain nothing more than a very small amount of tan powder. Their eyes met, then returned to the box. They were frightened by the death of their driver, now lying on the floor in the back room where they had carried him. Save for a small cut on his hand he appeared unharmed. *What had killed him?* The men shifted nervously around the object of their attention, but no words were spoken.

Ben, the leader of the group, did not like the situation at all. He was not a revolutionary. He was not even a patriot. He was a businessman, so when the representative of Fath had approached him with such a stupendous offer to smuggle in one small crate he had no choice but to accept. But now, an Israeli patrol had been attacked. "What if witnesses remained?" he thought. "And what about the dead driver?" His was a clandestine business, and he knew the risks. This time however, he did not feel in control. There were just too many questions. What was this shipment for the revolutionaries? Was it a weapon better that guns and explosives? Why was Fath willing to pay so dearly for it? How could it be so powerful?

Ibn Nimr received the message and his eyes shut momentarily. The destruction of Israel was at hand. Allah had answered his prayers, and he would prove himself worthy of the honor. He and his followers were truly members of a Master race. Finishing the note, he read the demand for payment of the final portion before delivery would be made. It was an astronomical sum. So great in fact that none of his usual supporters were willing to provide the funds. It was for this reason that he had made the decision nearly a year ago to begin using Fath to move drugs. Ibn Nimr was a devout Muslim, and dealing in heroin presented him with a moral dilemma. As a teenager he had smoked his share of hash-hish, but heroin controlled a person's mind, his life, and Allah was not served by it. However there simply was no other way to get the money to pay his Russian "friends." At times when he was alone, away from the blind adulation of his Fath followers, Ibn wondered who he actually hated more–his historic enemies, the Jews, or the Russians, who mocked his faith by forcing him to deal narcotics. Perhaps...perhaps he hated himself, because he allowed his ambition to compromise his faith. The only rationalization he had was that the drugs he trans-shipped would ultimately find their way to New York, where they would strike down more than a few of the American infidels.

"Comrade Kostyakova, I regret to inform you that the traitors appear to have eluded us," said Kazarian. "My officers arrested Skurnik and his family and as you predicted, those Samizdat pigs were helping them. At first they denied it, but with a little 'encouragement'," Kazarian's mouth stretched into a broad grin, "they confessed that they had put them on a flight to Berlin."

"You idiot!" screamed Kostyakova. "How could you let them get on that flight? And what are you grinning at? Did you enjoy your 'interrogations' that much? I should have you tortured, for a change. Then perhaps you would be able to focus more on your assignment, than on your fetishes."

"Let me think," said Kostyakova as he stared at the floor. "We must inform our American contact. We will need help in stopping this Colonel Rawlins."

In his corporate office at Unex, Grant Simms eased back in his Italian leather chair and took a sip of Chivas. His mind wandered off to his vacation next week in St. Maarten. *Ten million dollars.* His only problem now would be having to show a little discretion. Even an executive like himself probably wouldn't...

"Mr. Simms you have a call from Russia on five," breathed the sexy voice of his secretary, Cherie.

"Russia!" he blurted out, as the sexually explicit response he had intended for Cherie froze on his lips. His glass rolled to a stop on the antique Persian rug several feet away. *I can't believe...*"This is Simms. Just what in the hell do you think you are doing, calling me here?"

"I sincerely regret any inconvenience, Mr. Simms, but we have a problem. An American intelligence officer, a Colonel Rawlins, recently paid an unannounced visit to our facility, and now is making an effort to disrupt our business arrangement. Besides the obvious financial implications, the potential exists for one or both of us to become implicated in a very awkward situation—you understand. I was hoping your influence might help us...ameliorate this situation."

"Damn!" cursed Simms. "OK, wait, let's see, first of all, don't talk about this to anyone, ANYONE, do you hear? And don't call me here anymore. I'll get a hold of some people in Washington and we'll deal with this. I'll call you for more information later. Just stay where I can reach you and don't do anything, do you understand?"

The shipment began a circuitous and completely unchallenged journey, courtesy of official diplomatic pouches. From the Lebanese consulate in St. Petersburg it flew to the Lebanese Embassy in Paris, where it was transferred to the Libyan Embassy and flown directly to Tripoli. In Tripoli a senior political officer took personal charge of the shipment and carried it away in the trunk of his Mercedes. At his residence, the political officer transferred the box to a white minivan and drove it to the seaport, where it was handed over to the captain of a small tanker, just minutes before the vessel got underway for Greece, Cyprus and points east.

"Nick? Grant Simms. How are you doing? Listen, I need your help. We have a little problem with one of our international clients. You know the arrangement with Kirishi? Well it was going well until somehow one of the spooks from DIA, a Colonel Rawlins, got involved. He's loose somewhere between Berlin and I would guess Tel Aviv, and could quite possibly blow the whole deal. He needs to be stopped."

Nick DiGeorge, a U.S. security specialist assigned to Interpol, knew clearly what Simms meant. A supercop by anyone's standards, DiGeorge had been quietly paid a very large personal retainer to insure that this particular business deal was successful. He needed no convincing that Rawlins had to be stopped, and he needed no advice on how to do it.

"OK, Grant, just relax. I'll take care of it. Now, I'm going to need some information."

Chapter 15

"Welcome to Berlin, Mr. Whitesides. How long will you be staying in Germany?" asked the pert blond customs agent.

Zack stared blankly at her for a moment. "Pardon?"

"Your stay in Germany–how long?" she repeated cordially.

Percy Whitesides fell into character. "Terribly sorry. I'm just about all in, after that flight from St. Petersburg. I'll only be staying overnight."

"I know what you mean," said the agent. "Aeroflot passengers often show up here looking a bit...rumpled."

It dawned on Rawlins that he had not once seen himself in a mirror since changing clothes at Skurnik's house. He had been so distracted on the flight from St. Petersburg that he only now noticed what he was wearing. His yellowish shirt, tucked into baggy, black wool pants with no belt, was set off by a crimson satin tie. The outfit was completed by a brown tweed coat with leather elbow patches, for that avant-garde look.

"Christ," he thought to himself. "I look like a homeless person from D.C. If she buys this British Petroleum Company executive bullshit, I'm gonna be real surprised."

The customs agent stared at Rawlins for a moment, then noticed the long line forming as impatient passengers from three more jumbo jets surged into the arrival area. She looked back briefly at the man in front of her, who had the worst British accent she had ever heard, and shoved his documents back to him.

"Have a good day, Mr. Whitesides."

"Jolly good. Thank you. I'll be off, then," said Percy, and he hurried out into the terminal.

A brief telephone call to the political section at the U.S. embassy brought swift action. Zack had barely met back up with Petrenko at the baggage claim section when a smartly dressed woman approached them.

"Colonel Rawlins? I'm Julia Smith, regional affairs officer with the U.S. embassy," as she flashed her I.D. card. "I have a car waiting outside. You must be Colonel Petrenko. We'll get you both fixed up at the embassy, and have a doctor look at your injury. Colonel Rawlins, General Carter will be waiting for your call as soon as we get there."

Captain Steinberg strained his eyes through the helicopter canopy, looking for Mossat-Bar settlement. The chopper could not reach its rated speed because of the two bulky chemical pods attached to each side. With a payload of nearly five hundred gallons of antisense DNA solution, he could easily saturate an area twice the size of Mossat-Bar. The question was, would it work? In the laboratory his antisense technique was very impressive, but it had never been field tested. Likewise he had tried the technique in animals as a vaccine with astounding success, but had not yet gained approval for human trials.

The helo passed over a ridge and dropped down into the valley where Mossat-Bar lay.

"OK," Steinberg instructed the pilot. "We'll make north-south passes over the settlement, starting with those orchards to the west, until we cover everything east to the road. Come in low and slow at about fifty meters."

As they began each pass, Steinberg activated the sprayers. The heavy emulsion vortexed out in a fine mist behind the chopper, quickly settling to earth. After each pass he checked for the oily glint of the liquid covering their previous track. Finishing their coverage of the settlement, they repeated the pattern in an east-west direction.

"That should do it," said the Captain. "Nowhere to run, nowhere to hide, you little bastards."

"Minister Shoram," called Arielle Raebel, "Mr. Revich from Internal Affairs would like to speak with you. He's outside now."

"Send him in."

"Good afternoon, Sir. I just received a report that Dov Messer was killed in a car accident a few hours ago."

"What?" cried the Minister. "Now what will we…"

"Sir," interrupted Revitch. "Messer was carrying a Lebanese passport and papers that identified him as Ahmed Al-Habar."

Back at Lab 5, the staff was beginning to make some progress. The busywork that Dov had assigned them was completed, and now they had shifted to other tests and recovery routines that were finally bringing some systems back on line. The damage was immense though, with full operational capacity still several days away, and the Minister was demanding hourly status reports.

Even before the first shipment had left Kirishi, Nayah Salim had departed for Lebanon. With a forged diplomatic passport she had no trouble leaving Russia, or passing via a circuitous route to her native country. Kostyakova had ordered her not to leave the laboratory, but she insisted her work there was done, and she wanted to join the struggle with Fath. She had heard much about Ibn Nimr, the group's charismatic leader, and felt called to serve him.

In the small Lebanese village that hid the Fath headquarters, Nayah finally was escorted to meet the leader.

"I have been expecting you, Nayah," said Ibn Nimr. "You are well, I trust?"

"Yes, *ilhamdulillah*," she replied.

Nayah felt strongly attracted to the leader. Not only was he a handsome man, but he represented such confidence and power that she knew immediately that he would succeed. The destruction of Israel was at hand.

"The shipment arrived?" she asked.

"Yes, half of it is now with our people in Haifa, and the other half will arrive soon. I am leaving tonight to personally direct Operation Majdi. Will you accompany me?"

"I would be honored," replied Nayah.

Using his Interpol connections, it did not take Nick DiGeorge long to track Rawlins. Ironically, he activated the police system by a phony request for help in apprehending a fugitive heroin dealer. The confession "volunteered" by Vitaly Skurnik with the encouragement of Major Kazarian blew Rawlin's cover and pinpointed his arrival in Berlin. The information was passed to DiGeorge in London by the Moscow Interpol office.

"Damn!" cursed DiGeorge as he read the report on his secure teletype. Rawlins and Petrenko had already been on the ground in Berlin for several hours. They would have contacted the U.S. embassy by now, which meant they would have new passports. Petrenko would be no problem. DiGeorge knew the Russian was wounded and that the embassy would by now have him in a safe house. Rawlins however was a loose cannon. With his black diplomatic passport, and unknown orders from General Carter, the Colonel could be on his way back to Washington, or out chasing bad guys in Israel or even back in Russia.

When DiGeorge spoke with Grant Simms over a Unex company encrypted line, the executive told him for the first time that the high-value shipment he was "marketing" in the U.S. was heroin that originated in the Middle East. Money from the drug sales, well over ten million dollars, would pay off Kostyakova and DiGeorge, and ensure that Simms would never have to work another day in his life. Simms figured Kostyakova was probably supplying his Middle Eastern associate with some sort of weapons, but he never asked. It wasn't his concern. He only knew that the Russian shipment had to reach its buyer on time, or there would be a very unhappy customer, and a dissatisfied customer could complain very loudly.

In Kirishi, the Director wasted no time in shipping the other crate. This would close the deal, but more importantly, he could not allow any of the material to be found at the Institute. Now it all depended on Grant Simms. Stopping Colonel Rawlins meant the difference between retirement in a plush dacha on the Caspian, and life imprisonment in a Siberian labor camp.

Kostyakova summoned Dr. Steklov to his office, to instruct him on how he would deal with the "tragedy" at the laboratory.

"Dr. Steklov," stated the Director in an emotionless voice, "the five employees who died were overcome by toxic chemical gasses from a ruptured reactor, during processing of agrochemicals. You are to totally decontaminate the containment level 4 facility and autoclave everything in it including the corpses. All laboratory records and notebooks are to be incinerated. Then you will immediately convert the facility to the production of additional single cell protein. I want this done in forty-eight hours. Do you understand my orders?"

"Yes, Comrade Kostyakova," stammered the Chief Scientist. *Chemical gasses? How could he face the families of the workers with such a story?* Steklov had no trouble however with following the orders to decontaminate the laboratory. He knew the truth about the accident, and understood that without absolute sterilization of the laboratory and its contents, those valuable, high-tech work spaces could never be safely used again for any purpose.

As his Mercedes sped south toward Haifa, Ibn Nimr discussed the operation with Nayah. Lebanon, Syria and Jordan had coordinated the placement of over three hundred SCUD-B rockets near their borders with Israel. These rockets, equipped with both chemical and high explosive warheads, could strike anywhere in the country. Although positioning of the mobile launchers had been done quickly, during nighttime hours, their movements were never meant to be entirely clandestine. The missiles were, in fact, a diversionary tactic. The attackers hoped to focus Israel's attention on the peripheral threat of the missiles, while Fath struck at Israel's heart.

"We perhaps underestimated the Zionist response," acknowledged Ibn Nimr, referring to the ten-megaton wake-up call some of his fighters received in the Bekaa Valley. "A minor tactical error, but our strategy remains sound."

Nayah simply stared at the Fath leader in rapt amazement. This man was God-like. A successful nuclear strike against his allies was dismissed as "a minor tactical error." Israel could launch more nuclear weapons at any time, while a barrage of SCUDs could turn Israel's major cities into toxic rubble. Through all this Ibn Nimr focused with crystal clarity only on his mission. In fact, he was far from a god. To the hostile nations surrounding Israel, Ibn Nimr was little more than a cipher. His main value was his organization, Fath, which enjoyed widespread support in the occupied territories bordering Israel and maintained a network of collaborators inside of the country. Nimr even boldly made his home in Tel Aviv, where he lived a double life as a Lebanese businessman with his family, while directing his clandestine operation.

"We have targeted every major water distribution point in Israel," said Ibn Nimr. "Within twenty four hours, every Jew who touches or drinks water from a public system will be exposed. We have calculated a seventy five percent mortality within two days. This number of casualties will overwhelm the hospitals, cripple all industry and the military and bring Israel to its knees." The Fath leader was unaware that the biological weapon he possessed had mutated, and now would kill anyone infected by it. "Lebanon, Syria and Jordan will then demand an unconditional surrender and assume joint control of the country. If there is any organized resistance, or any hesitation by whatever government authority remains, SCUDs will pound them into submission."

The car phone rang, and Ibn Nimr answered impatiently, "Yes?"

Nayah watched, as Ibn's face became somber. She picked up clipped conversation, "When, where are they now?"

Ibn replaced the phone and stared out the window. "Rorsha's security forces picked up my wife and daughter at the Tel Aviv airport as they were leaving for Damascus. They are being detained somewhere in the city."

Nayah reacted, "Operation Majdi. How can we now continue?"

Ibn continued to stare through the window, and didn't answer. His decision was already made.

Zack Rawlins' orders from General Carter were simple and direct. Get to Israel and intercept the BW shipments before they could be deployed. The Colonel was personally authorized by the Israeli Defense Minister to use any method at his disposal to carry out his mission. There simply was no time to organize a military response, it was going to be Zack's show.

At Tel Aviv airport, Zack's El Al jet stopped on the taxiway, where it was met by an Israeli military jeep. The flight crew, obeying orders radioed to them by airport control, opened the aircraft exit door and deployed the emergency slide. In seconds, Zack was in the jeep, racing toward the defense ministry. On the vehicle's radio, he spoke with Minister Shoram.

"What's the picture, Minister Shoram?" he asked.

"We have not retaliated further, yet," replied the DM. "However we are surrounded by SCUD-Bs, and we believe they are armed with the BW agent. We cannot allow these weapons to be used against Israel, and we are prepared for a full scale nuclear response against Lebanon, Syria and Jordan."

"Minister Shoram," pleaded Rawlins, "don't launch your nukes. Your neighbors are taking a terrible gamble, but it's part of a greater plan. Those SCUDs are an extremely serious threat, but their deployment is a diversion. They are not armed with the BW agent used against your settlements. The BW is in two shipments of small ampoules that have just arrived in your country. I believe they are to be distributed to key points around Israel and then used to contaminate the water supply. The two cases must be found before their contents are distributed. Once it gets in the water supply, Israel will have no potable water."

With the help of Kostyakova, DiGeorge was able to get a message to Fath headquarters. At the risk of being intercepted by Israeli electronic surveillance, the message was then relayed to Ibn Nimr by car phone, where he and Nayah Salim were speeding toward Haifa, to the house where the weapon was stored. The message was clear and simple. An American intelligence officer, Colonel Zachary Rawlins, was in Tel Aviv. It was believed he knew details of Operation Majdi and his mission was to intercept and stop the planned BW attack. He was to be neutralized, at all costs.

Simultaneously, DiGeorge would coordinate an Interpol action against Rawlins, under the ruse of apprehending an armed and dangerous international drug dealer. During his apprehension, the suspect would be killed while "resisting arrest."

The driver impatiently sounded his horn, but drew no response at the gate of the house. With a concerned glance into the rearview mirror back at the Fath leader, he removed the pistol from his shoulder holster and opened the door of the Mercedes. Peering cautiously over the gate, he saw the first body sprawled on the driveway. Lights shone through the windows of the house, and the front door stood half open, but he saw no one else.

Turning toward the car, he gestured for his passengers to wait, and then reached over the gate to release the latch. Slowly opening the gate, he disappeared inside. In less than a minute he returned with the report that there were several bodies inside, but no sign of a fight.

"Wait," cautioned Nayah, as Ibn reached for the door handle. "I don't think we should go in there now."

Ibn Nimr ignored the woman, slipped from the car and strode into the house. Inside, he assessed the situation. Five bodies, no sign of a struggle. On the table in the living room sat the first shipment, intact except for what appeared to be some minor damage to the box and a few broken vials. The second shipment had also arrived, sitting on the floor next to the wall, and appeared undamaged.

"Ibn?" called Nayah, peering in through the front doorway.

"Wait in the car," ordered the Fath leader. "I must think. *Majdi* cannot be delayed."

"I know women are not fighters," said Nayah, "but I created this weapon. Please let me help. We must work quickly and, as you can see, we must be extremely careful."

"Our fallen brothers here were assigned to deliver the weapon to specific water distribution points throughout Israel. Their martyrdom is recognized by Allah, but the timetable of Operation Majdi is now compromised. I am afraid we must strike the first blow ourselves, or the Zionists may prevail."

"Quickly, take the box from the table and put it in the car. I'll bring the other. We will poison the water of Tel Aviv and then call in missiles. With the help of Allah, we will still succeed."

At Fath headquarters, Ibn Nimr's call alerted the organization of his change in plans. He would go personally to the main water distribution center on the outskirts of Tel Aviv, where Fath collaborators would neutralize the security forces, and contaminate the city's water supply. Before the government could react, or spread any warning, there would be hundreds of thousands of casualties. In the chaos that followed, SCUD missiles launched from Syria and Lebanon would saturate the capitol with a massive chemical and high explosives attack.

Fath headquarters acknowledged and agreed to the plan. There was really no alternative now if Operation Majdi were to succeed, but Ibn Nimr was warned of the presence of the American intelligence officer in country whose mission was to stop him at all costs.

In the city, Zack had correctly reasoned that the terrorists would strike at the water distribution center, and that their actions would be coordinated with a SCUD attack, but he couldn't call in Israeli Special Forces. It was possible that Fath had already taken the pump house, but not yet contaminated the water. One man might have a chance of getting inside unnoticed and stopping the mission, but a massive show of Israeli force would surely panic the fanatics into executing their orders prematurely.

As Zack tried to focus on a plan, he saw the face of his beautiful niece, Sarah. Her soft, trusting brown eyes were looking up at her mother, as she was handed a big glass of water to drink, somewhere in Tel Aviv. "Goddammit!" he cursed. "Those sons of bitches!"

Fath had also relayed the change in the situation to Nick DiGeorge, who had taken the first available flight to Tel Aviv. Racing from the airport in his rental car, DiGeorge sped toward the water distribution center. His intuition told him that he would find Rawlins there, and he would make sure that the American was no longer a problem. The third member of the deadly meeting, Ibn Nimr, closed in from the north on the water distribution center, unaware of the other players in the final act.

At the pumping station, Fath gunmen easily overwhelmed the civil servants operating the facility. When the Fath leader arrived at the gate, they hurried his car inside.

"Allahuahkbar," breathed Ibn. "Come, Nayah, let us put your weapon to the test."

Zack drove slowly by the main gate of the pumping facility. The guard house was conspicuously unmanned.

"He's here. No time to wait. Gotta get in there now."

Turning quickly around behind the facility he stopped by a storage shed against the back wall. In a moment Zack was on top of the shed, peering cautiously over the wall into the compound. Seeing no one in the yard, he slipped over the wall and dropped ten feet to the ground inside.

Unknown to Zack, Nick DiGeorge was just pulling up at the front gate of the facility, missing him by seconds. With no response to his car horn, DiGeorge jumped out and repeatedly pressed the call button beside the gate.

The gate opened slightly and a heavily armed man asked suspiciously, *Ayiz eh*? "What do you want?"

"Ibn Nimr," answered DiGeorge, "I must see Ibn Nimr immediately. Tell him I am from New York and I am here to protect our investment."

The gate closed, and after what seemed an interminable delay, the armed man returned and opened the gate, this time his Uzi at the ready.

"Come, Ibn Nimr will see you."

Behind the main pumphouse, Zack tried every door including the large loading dock roll door, but all were locked. The high pitched roar of the main water pumps made it difficult to think clearly. Zack's stomach tightened as he visualized hundreds of glass vials of the deadly bacteria smashing through the turbine blades, their lethal contents squirting out under the tremendous water pressure, into the mouths of millions of unsuspecting men, women and children.

Leaning over the railing on the edge of the loading dock, Rawlins peered in through an open window and saw two men and a woman in intense conversation. The tall Arab was most likely Ibn Nimr, and Zack guessed the woman was Nayah Salim. The other man looked western, but was no one he recognized. As the three argued excitedly, Zack noticed them repeatedly gesturing toward the object of their attention, two cardboard cases on the floor next to the water turbines.

"The shipments," he gasped. "They haven't used the bugs yet." Zack wanted to leap through the window and seize the cases of BW. He still had a chance of stopping them, although without any sort of weapon it was a very small chance. At that moment, one of the Fath gunmen had the misfortune of rounding the corner of the pumphouse, and making the acquaintance of Colonel Zachary Rawlins, United States Army. Zack thanked him for the Uzi, and the extra bonus of two hand grenades, but the prone form didn't respond.

Back at the defense ministry, Shoram stared nervously at General Morah, then raised the red telephone and keyed the call button.

"Arm three missiles. Target Damascus, Beirut and Amman. Wait for my orders. I want all Patriot anti-missile batteries fully mobilized. Scramble one fighter and two bomber wings. Ben, I think we can take out about a third of the SCUDs on the ground, and the Patriots should intercept about half of those remaining, but we're going to take some serious damage in Tel Aviv and Haifa. The only decision now is whether or not to strike first."

"I say nuke the bastards now," growled the General. "Not just because that will give me tremendous satisfaction, but also because it should disrupt command and control of the SCUD attacks, and limit the effectiveness of their strike."

"However if Colonel Rawlins can abort the BW attack," countered the DM, "our enemies may think twice about initiating the conventional strike. They know that without a successful two-pronged attack Israel will prevail, and turn them all into nuclear rubble."

"And I say the time has come to do exactly that. Our people are facing annihilation, and we cannot wait. We don't dare take the chance. These are not rational people," argued the General.

The DM stared into the deep red and brown colors of his carpet and saw millions of people incinerated on his orders. *Not rational people...they aren't even people.*

"Ben, call Zev Rorsha and give Special Forces the go-ahead at the pumping station. I know Rawlins said to hold off, but if he fails, we launch."

Still considering his options, Rawlins peered back through the window and froze. Ibn Nimr and the westerner had climbed to the catwalk alongside the main pumps, and the roar of the turbines screamed through the open, three-foot access port. Each man held one case of the BW agent, and they clearly were preparing to dump the contents into the water system. His options now severely restricted, Zack pulled the pin on one of his grenades, placed it at the base of the large roll door and jumped off the loading dock.

The blast tore a five foot hole through the door, and Rawlins leaped through. Nayah Salim cringed below the catwalk, staring open-mouthed up at Ibn Nimr. The two men looked at Rawlins and spun around, their deadly cargoes directed at the open maw of the pump, inches away. With no time to think, Zack unleashed a burst from his Uzi, which caught the first man full in the chest. The case fell from his hands to the catwalk grating and he pitched violently backward, disappearing through the access port into the spinning blades of the high speed turbine. The pump shuddered only slightly, as it processed DiGeorge into a protein-rich suspension to fortify the water supply of Tel Aviv.

Ibn Nimr raised the second case over his head and shouted, "Allahuahkbar!"

"Only one chance, you son-of-a-bitch," cursed Rawlins, as he emptied his clip at the Fath leader.

"Ibn Nimr convulsed as bullets tore through his body and through the case, pitching him backward off the catwalk. He crashed down directly onto Nayah Salim, in a shower of glass shards that pierced her skin a hundred times."

The front door of the pumphouse burst open and Fath gunmen poured in behind a hail of automatic weapon fire. Zack greeted them with his last grenade, but was slammed to the floor by the impact of several slugs. Consciousness fading, he thought he heard the sound of helicopter gunships followed by explosions and the hum of Gatling mini-guns, then it was dark.

Chapter 16

"Minister Shoram," reported General Morah, "Special Forces has secured the water distribution facility. It appears that Fath failed to contaminate the water supply."

"Thank God," cried the Minister. "And Colonel Rawlins?"

"He's been wounded," replied the General. "I don't know his condition yet. They're medevacing him now."

"What about the BW agent?"

"The ERT is on the scene. They have isolated the entire facility and are decontaminating it with the anti-sense DNA formulation that cleaned up Mossat-Bar."

The DM slumped in his chair, then looked up and grinned at General Morah. "We did it, Ben, we did it! Put the nukes on standby, but at full alert. Keep the air wings up. Get me an emergency conference call with the Defense Ministers of Syria, Lebanon and Jordan. Tell them they better replace those SCUDs with marshmallows and kosher hotdogs, because we're ready to roast."

Nayah Salim was easily captured without serious injury by the Israeli Special Forces, but within half an hour, the overwhelming dose of BW agent she had received from the shower of broken ampoules at the pumping station took its course. With virtually every muscle in her body tetanizing, she was gripped by acute respiratory failure. The hyper-contracted masseter muscles of the jaw drew her face into a contorted, sardonic smile, as her captors helplessly watched her life extinguish.

In Russian, the net closed quickly on Kostyakova. Based on information from General Carter, the American Ambassador detailed the events to General Vankovich, who ordered the Director's arrest. After that the dominoes fell quickly. Major Kazarian was rounded up and interrogated, and he soon revealed the prison locations of Boris Dutrev, as well as Vitaly Skurnik and his family.

Documents found in DiGeorge's rental car implicated Grant Simms at Unex, and U.S. federal agents quickly moved to modify his vacation plans from St. Maarten to a much less sunny place.

Chapter 17

Rawlin's eyes opened slightly, then closed, then opened again, as he tested reality. *Shapes, human shapes.*

"Zack, Zack I'm here, darling," soothed Sally's voice.

Slowly his mind began to integrate and his eyes opened wide.

"You look like shit!" boomed the familiar voice of General Carter.

Zack lay motionless, his eyes shifting between the two figures leaning over each side of his bed, and a weak smile spread across his face. He did not know where he was, only that he was alive and safe, with the two most influential people in his life standing guard over him. As he focused on Sally's face, a silent vow joined them. This was his last mission–they both knew it, and they both meant it. He tried to speak but his voice would not cooperate, so he responded with his left hand in a feeble thumbs-up. Rawlins focused on a third figure at the foot of his bed, the grinning face of Monty Rodriguez.

"Welcome back, Sir. Boy, what some people won't do for another medal."

The Colonel looked quizzically at General Carter, who held up a small awards case to reveal a bronze medal on a red and white ribbon, the Legion of Merit.

"Zack, I just want you to know I appreciate what you've done. If that bug had gotten loose it would have killed millions, and destabilized the entire Middle East. Because of you, all the countries involved in this mess realize what a close call this was for all humanity, and they have agreed to meet immediately for multi-lateral peace talks." Bending over Rawlins, the General fumbled with the hospital gown as he tried to affix the medal with its pin.

Zack's lights were going back out, and he mumbled something silly about a tetanus booster if the General stuck him.

"You know, Sally," said General Carter, "Zack should take some time off, go fishing in Vermont or something. He's really been working too hard lately." Carter had intended the remark as a joke, but he had caught the look shared by Sally and Zack, and he knew the Colonel was already gone.

Printed in the United States
25037LVS00005B/37-45

9 780595 098170